GROUND TO A HALT

Elaine Orr

Copyright © 2014 Elaine L. Orr

All rights reserved.

ISBN: 150586805X
ISBN-13: 978-1505868050

DEDICATION

To Wayne and Carol Orr, family treasures.

GROUND TO A HALT

Elaine Orr

Large Print Edition

Copyright 2014 by Elaine L. Orr

Scoobie's poetry by James W. Larkin

This Create Space edition is licensed for your personal use.

www.elaineorr.com

www.elaineorr.blogspot.com

ACKNOWLEDGMENTS

Thanks to my sister Diane, who always offers helpful comments. I wrote much of this book in the Starbucks on Freedom Drive in Springfield, Illinois. Staff were friendly and good-humored, even when I spilled coffee. Lorena Shute provided her usual eagle eye as a copyeditor. As always, thanks to my husband, Jim, for understanding the schedule I keep when I write.

CHAPTER ONE

THE MIDDLE-OF-THE-NIGHT thunderstorm meant no electricity. That translated to no alarm clock, no hair dryer, and no coffee. And me being late.

Since most Jersey shore businesses have backup generators, I jogged up the steps to the Ocean Alley boardwalk. It was empty at six-forty-five on a crisp, mid-October morning. Good. I wanted a cup of Java Jolt coffee to take to the house I was to appraise, and didn't want to wait in line. Why someone wanted a real estate appraiser at seven-fifteen I couldn't imagine, but there you go.

Java Jolt doesn't open until seven o'clock, so I thought the door might be locked. It was ajar. Since Owner Joe Regan likely knew half of Ocean Alley had no power, he had probably come in early.

I pushed open the glass door and sniffed in anticipation. But no coffee aroma wafted toward me. Nuts. Too early.

"Hey, Joe. First customer."

Silence. I glanced around the small shop. Joe made a lot of repairs after Hurricane Sandy. In addition to new paneling and chairs, he'd moved the counter back a few feet so there could be more tables. I liked the look.

I leaned on the counter, almost knocking over the honor sugar bowl that customers use for payment when it's not tourist season. Behind the counter was a small stock room. Down the short hall was a unisex bathroom. Joe, known for his sometimes grouchy manner, would not appreciate being dethroned, so to speak.

"Joe?" I pushed my still-damp, shoulder length brown hair behind my ears and glanced in the mirror behind the counter. I definitely looked like a woman who had dressed in near dark. The collar of my purple polo shirt was up in the back, and I straightened it.

I thought about leaving and grabbing coffee at the convenience mart, but something didn't feel right.

At the side of the counter farthest from the boardwalk entrance is a fairly narrow opening that allows Joe and other coffee servers to get to their work area behind the counter. I moved that way, glancing around Java Jolt as I did so. Where is he? Maybe he's just taking out garbage.

I moved along the counter on the worker side and got to the storeroom. Joe had made it smaller after the storm. I peered in. Nothing there but shelves of coffee, napkins, sugar, and such. The narrow hall to the restroom was just behind the store room. I leaned my head around the door jamb, feeling uncertain about whether I should walk down the hall.

Don't be ridiculous.

Instead of coffee brewing, the smell that greeted me was that of a cool breeze. The back door had to be open. Maybe Joe was in the alley immediately behind the shop.

"Joe?"

I walked to the end of the short hallway that ended in a T,

which had really short ends on the crossbar. To the left was the exit door. It was closed but not latched, and fluttered open and shut an inch or two in the breeze. A glance through the glass on the door did not reveal Joe in the alley.

On the floor was a zippered bank deposit bag, which was partially open. Next to it were an order book and pencil stub.

"This is not good." I stooped to reach for the money bag, then thought better of it and stood.

The voice behind me was strident. "What are you doin'?"

I turned, bumping my elbow on the hallway wall. "I just…Sergeant Morehouse!"

"Jolie?" He stared at me. "You the one who called?"

"No, I just came in for coffee. No one's here."

Morehouse spoke into a small radio. "Yeah, I stopped by. Place is open, no sign of Joe." He listened for a second. "I dunno. If it's clearin' up on E Street send someone over."

I studied him as he clipped the radio back on his belt. Morehouse is about ten or twelve years older than my age of thirty-one. He usually wears solid-color ties, white or pastel-colored shirts, and polyester pants. Combine that with his closely cropped brown hair and he looks kind of like police detectives in a TV show from the early 1970s. Now, however, he wore a dark green knit shirt and deck shoes. Not exactly regulation police wear.

We both said, "Where's Joe?"

"You bein' the one in here, I'm thinkin' you would know," he said.

I shook my head. "I'm only here this early because my electricity's off. The front door was open." I nodded toward the door that exited onto the alley. "This one, too."

He motioned me toward him, and I had to turn sideways to

walk around him so he could move through the hall and look around. I stood near the coffee counter and watched him open the door to the bathroom and what looked like a mop closet.

He frowned. "Half the town's out. Storm came through about four." He got to where the narrow hallway turned toward the back exit and looked down at the bank bag.

I nodded. "I heard the thunder, but I didn't know power was out until this morning."

"Go back out to the customer area and try not to touch anything." He looked up at the ceiling and down the hall. "Some of our guys should be here in a minute. Three-car fender bender on E Street, near In-Town Market."

I folded my arms across my chest and walked into the area where customers sit. Surely Joe will be here any minute. I wanted to call my best bud—and now boyfriend—Scoobie, but he wouldn't know anything about Joe. The call would be to reassure me.

Scoobie had given me a quick kiss as he left the house at six-fifteen. It was a big day. In honor of it, he had on new maroon hospital scrubs, and his dark blonde hair and beard were neatly trimmed. After eighteen months of training at the community college, today was Scoobie's first day in his new job as a radiology technician at Ocean Alley Hospital. The last thing he needed was a call about Joe's whereabouts.

Morehouse walked to the counter and I asked, "Why did you come?"

He stared across the counter at me, frowning. "Got a call the door was open and Joe wasn't here. They called me at home 'cause everyone's tied up with traffic and a couple of business alarms that won't go off."

"Who called?"

Morehouse's response was testy. "Some customer doing what you were. Don't matter."

I walked to the window and looked onto the boardwalk. "Where could he be?"

"Like I know. If you don't know nuthin', head outside."

I nodded toward the back of the coffee shop. "It's not good that the bank deposit bag is on the floor."

Morehouse gave me one of his I-wish-I-didn't-know-you looks and I walked to the door. "I have to do an appraisal at seven-fifteen. I'm leaving."

Morehouse was back on his radio and ignored me. I walked out and glanced up and down the boardwalk. People were out now, and the owner of the French Fries shop was unlocking her door. She's one of the last boardwalk businesses to close each fall, and just had her clapboard store painted hot pink. It looked garish next to the lime green of the cotton candy store next to it.

The breeze was from the land and brisk. That and stiff white-caps were reminders of the recent storm.

If it had been early May instead of October, more people would be around, but Ocean Alley is generally only super crowded from May to mid-September. With a resident population of twenty thousand and no casino, it's too small to attract much off-season excitement. We residents like that.

What would make Joe leave like that? I had no idea whether he made his deposits at night or in the morning, so didn't know how long the bank bag had been on the floor. On the other hand, the doors were both ajar, and I didn't see water on the floor. It seemed more likely that he'd been in his shop after the morning storm.

My mobile phone chirped and I glanced at the caller ID.

My boss. "Hi, Harry. Checking to see if I'm up?"

Harry Steele owns the smaller of Ocean Alley's two real estate appraisal firms, and I'm his only employee. He opened the business after he retired and moved to Ocean Alley, and has no intention to grow it. Though he's her junior by more than ten years, Harry married Aunt Madge, who's in her early eighties, about eighteen months ago. It doesn't interfere in our business relationship. It might if I still lived in her Cozy Corner B&B, but I'm happily ensconced in the small bungalow I bought almost a year ago.

"Not that I doubt you, but I didn't know if you had a clock that wasn't electric."

"I do. I'm out getting coffee and I'll get there by seven-fifteen."

"Righto. Okay, I'm coming." The last phrase was addressed to Aunt Madge's two golden retrievers, Mister Rogers and Miss Piggy, whom I could hear whimpering in the background. Harry has become their morning walker. "Gotta go."

I stuck the phone in the side pocket of my navy blue capri pants and walked off the boardwalk. I needed to put Joe out of my mind and hustle to the job.

THE INTERIOR OF the house on Fairweather Street could be described as fussy. Every surface boasted knick knacks, and throw rugs dotted the beige carpet, which looked new. Owner Mortimer Fielding was also fussy.

Before I could say more than hello, he said, "I need you out of here by eight o'clock. I have a real estate agent coming then, and I want you to tell me what the house is worth before he gets here." Fielding was a compact man in his early seventies, and his protruding ear hair was as clean as a cotton ball. There was nothing fluffy about his tone.

I stared at him for a beat and took a breath. I figured I had one chance to make my point. "There is no way to tell you what your house is worth until I finish the appraisal, sir. You see…"

"So finish before eight, Miss Gentle."

"Gentil is pronounced Zhan-tee, soft G, long E sound at the end. Soft J on Jolie, too."

Fielding eyed me as if I didn't know how to pronounce my own name.

"A key part of an appraisal is comparing your house to recent selling prices of similar houses in town. Otherwise we're looking at your house in a vacuum."

"A vacuum is fine," he snapped. "I just need to know what it's worth so I don't get screwed."

I thought for a moment. It seemed he thought a real estate agent would encourage him to price his house low. "I need to tell you two things."

His chin jutted forward, but Fielding said nothing.

"First, an agent makes more money when your house is priced higher, so no one wants a low price."

He frowned, backed up a step, and looked at me with skepticism.

"Second, what I'm here to do is measure your house and take photos. Then I'll go to the courthouse to see about comparably priced sales, and then I'll go photograph those houses to be sure they really are like yours. Then Harry Steele and I will give you our opinion about what your house is worth. That might be late today, or could be early tomorrow."

"That's more than two things."

"Yes, it is. Do you understand?"

"I'm not stupid."

"I didn't say you were." I held his gaze. "One final thing. I figured since you requested the appraisal rather than a bank that you were selling the house yourself. If you wait until you have a sales contract, the prospective buyer pays for the appraisal. If you do it now, you pay."

"Yeah, yeah. Harry Whatever told me that." He walked away from me, toward his kitchen.

Harry Whatever? I felt sorry for the agent who got this listing.

I took out my cloth tape measure. It's Aunt Madge's innovation, and combines a bunch of sewing tape measures. It's longer than any metal one, and less heavy. It would take me about twenty minutes to measure the three-bedroom house and jot notes. I'd have to take a lot of photos to justify a decent price.

Housing prices for property so close to the ocean have fluctuated widely. Depending on how a prospective buyer looked at it, Mr. Fielding was either three blocks from a fun day of sun and sand or in the path of a hurricane-generated storm surge.

The clock on his small mantle said seven-fifty when Mr. Fielding came in from the back yard, where he had apparently sought refuge from me. "You done?"

"I've finished interior photos, and I'll take several outside and be on my way."

"Humph. Make sure you get my maple tree. Leaves are real red now."

I told him I would, let myself out, and sat my purse and

notebook on the front steps. After snapping three pictures, a loud voice came from behind me. "Jolie. What the hell are you doin'?"

I turned to see Lester Argrow, the pushiest member of the Ocean Alley real estate cadre and occasional thorn in my side. Lester kind of looks like a stereotypical low-level mob guy. He's short with an unlit cigar hanging perpetually from his lip. He's only ten years older than I am, and his receding brown hair has just a touch of grey. He's also the uncle of my high school classmate and good friend Ramona, who sometimes wishes their last names were different.

"You're gonna tell the old buzzard his house is worth less than it should be."

"Who you callin' a buzzard?" Mr. Fielding stood on his front porch and glared at Lester, who now stood next to me on the small lawn.

I aimed my camera at the house and used it to hide my mouth. "You deserve each other," I murmured.

"Figure of speech, Mortimer." Lester waved to him and turned to me. "Call me before you and that lunkhead tell Mr. Fielding what you think."

Lunkhead? Harry and Lester are often at loggerheads about an appraisal. This does not happen with any other agent in Ocean Alley, because the others price a house realistically. Lester only thinks about his commission. It sounded as if their periodic disagreements had escalated to more serious name calling. On Lester's part, anyway.

I DROVE AROUND A UTILITY truck whose crew seemed to be working on a transformer and pulled into the parking lot of Mr. Markle's In-Town Market. He has a coffee

9

pot for customers, and I still hadn't had my morning dose of caffeine. Though he tends to grumble about it, Mr. Markle is always willing to sell the Harvest for All Food Pantry groceries at cost if we're out of a key item. This usually translates to green beans or breakfast cereal for kids. Since I chair the pantry oversight committee, which means fundraising arm, I'm grateful.

The sun was finally out and the last vestiges of the early morning storm were clouds on the eastern horizon. I took off my lightweight blue jacket as I walked from the parking lot to the store. It's not large. Most people shop at one of the bigger chain stores on the edge of town. Mr. Markle has a loyal clientele, many of them elderly patrons who no longer drive or prefer not to challenge tourists on the busy highway.

"Morning, Jolie." Mr. Markle was straightening the newspaper display near the cash register.

"You sound cheerful," I said.

"Generator kicked in like it was supposed to. Power just came back on, and the cars from that accident are finally all cleared away."

I helped myself to coffee from the card table near the door. "I heard about that. Was it a bad accident?"

"No, but one of the drivers ran off. Probably a kid."

I raised my cup as if toasting him. "Couldn't make coffee at home and had to be at an appraisal early."

"And here I thought you wanted to shop." He turned toward the register.

"I need a thing of coffee for home." I said this to his back and walked toward the rear of the store. I still had enough for a few days and it was cheaper elsewhere. I decided to think of the higher price of the ground coffee as the cost of the cup

I was drinking.

The selection is more limited at the In-Town Market, but there are several kinds and I stared at the shelf trying to decide if the generic of coffee brand was enough cheaper to make it a bargain. I looked up as the swinging doors to the back storeroom opened and Joe Regan walked through them. His auburn hair looked kind of mussed, and he was wearing the white apron he uses at Java Jolt.

Joe appeared as surprised to see me as I was to see him. "Uh, hi, Jolie."

"Hi. I'm glad you're okay."

Joe looked confused. "Okay?"

"I went to your store early. The door was open and…"

"Was anyone else there?"

I studied him for a few seconds. "Well, no. I mean, Sergeant Morehouse came in. Someone else called…"

"That's good," he said, quickly. "Listen, Jolie, I have stuff to do."

"Are you okay?"

He didn't answer. Rather than walk by me, Joe walked down the grocery aisle next to mine. His footsteps grew fainter, and I heard Mr. Markle call to him. I didn't hear Joe respond. That's odd.

I told myself I was not responsible for someone else's behavior, a lesson I continue to try to learn, and took the generic brand of coffee from the shelf. As I made my way to the front of the store I heard Mr. Markle's phone ring and listened to him assure a caller that he was open.

Mr. Markle finished checking out an older man I recognized as an occasional food pantry customer. Mr. Hanson, I thought.

He waved, and said, "Hello, Jolie. Probably see you later this month."

"You're always welcome," I said, and smiled.

Mr. Markle looked at me as I set my coffee on the conveyer belt. "You have a lot of elderly customers at the pantry?"

"Mostly at the end of the month." I took a five dollar bill from my purse. "How long was Joe Regan in here?"

"Joe? He just left. I didn't see him come in." He finished ringing the item and took my money.

"I, um, thought I saw him coming out of your storage area."

Mr. Markle shrugged. "I put supplies I order for him on a shelf. He was probably checking."

"Ah. Thanks. I'll likely see you later in the week."

"Tell Scoobie to come over. I have a box of dented cans."

"Thanks." I walked slowly to my car. I knew I should get right to the office, which is in the house Harry bought before he and Aunt Madge married. But maybe I should go to the police. Something told me they might consider Joe Regan to be some sort of missing person. I didn't want to mind Joe's business, but his expression said something wasn't right.

As I opened my car door I heard a pop. It wasn't as loud as a car backfire, but more than a kid would make squashing an aluminum can. Then there was another pop.

Joe Regan walked around the corner from Seashore Street, coming toward me. If he's coming back to the store he must be fine.

I thought that until Joe collapsed on the sidewalk.

CHAPTER TWO

INSTINCT PULLED ME toward and away from Joe. I wanted to help him, but my muddled thinking said the noise had been a gun. I compromised by crouching and looking toward Joe for several long seconds.

When there were no more ominous pops I stumbled toward him, leaning forward as I went. Some TV show must have taught me I'd be less of a target if I bent over.

Joe was on his side and his eyes were open. I knelt next to him, unsure what to do. *I need to call 9-1-1!* Sirens headed toward us made me drop the phone I'd just taken from my pocket and I looked at Joe. "Help is coming."

He whispered. "Jolie. Don't let them hurt him." He coughed and drew a raspy breath.

"Hurt who?"

Joe closed his eyes.

A heavy vehicle door slammed and two EMTs sprinted toward Joe and me. "Move back!"

I obeyed by falling from my squatting position onto my butt and kind of crab walking backwards for a few steps. I could only stare at Joe. He was so…white.

"Back, Jolie, back."

It was Sergeant Morehouse, now dressed for business.

Somehow I couldn't move any more. He reached down and yanked me into a standing position by grabbing my elbow. "What did you see?" he yelled.

I pointed to Joe and looked at Morehouse, still unable to speak.

He lowered his voice. "Are you hurt?"

"I…no. Joe, he came towards me…" I looked toward the corner of E and Seashore Street. There were several bright red spots on the sidewalk behind Joe. Blood?

Morehouse grabbed my elbow and moved me a couple meters away from Joe and the EMTs. "Did you see anyone with a gun?"

"No. I think…he was just around that corner." I gestured to the end of the street.

Morehouse pointed toward the corner and two uniformed officers who had been running toward us turned and ran with Morehouse in that direction. They ran to the right and disappeared.

"Jolie, come inside." Mr. Markle called from the door to the market. His tone was insistent.

I walked toward him and asked, "What happened?" I had seen Joe fall, it just didn't seem real.

A ledge runs at the bottom of the plate glass windows that face the street. Little kids try to walk on it and their parents shoo them off. Mr. Markle more or less pushed me to sit there and he walked to the coffee pot and poured me another cup.

"Thanks." I took a small sip, careful not to scald myself. Not until the hot liquid hit my throat did I realize I was shaking.

"You aren't going to hit the floor, are you?"

I looked up at Mr. Markle. He's about five-ten and kind of pear shaped. The front side of the pear is rounder than it was a few years ago. I couldn't help it. I started to giggle. I put my hand over my mouth. "I'm sorry. It's not funny."

He stared at me, both hands now on his hips. "You're in shock or something."

The whoosh of the hydraulic entry door made both of us turn in that direction. Sergeant Morehouse walked in with Dana Johnson, my favorite officer on the Ocean Alley Police Force, a couple of steps behind him.

Morehouse pointed at me. "You okay?"

I nodded as Mr. Markle said, "Jolie said earlier that she saw Joe coming out of my back storage area."

Dana started for the back of the store. Morehouse put the radio to his lips. "Check behind the store. Seems Joe was just in the store room." Someone on the other end of the radio crackled an okay.

Morehouse glanced toward Dana's back. "Wait up." Morehouse did a half-jog to catch up with her and they were soon out of sight.

I looked at Mr. Markle. "Thanks a lot."

"That's the third time you've thanked me today." He turned and walked a few feet from me to peer around the huge sale signs that covered the plate glass window. "Ambulance is gone."

"Do you think he'll be okay?"

Markle looked at me in mild irritation, and his expression softened a bit. "They left in a hurry. That's usually a good sign." He walked to the cash register to pick up his clip board and started writing on it.

How can he do normal work now?

Two more police officers came in, but they didn't look to be in a particular hurry. They looked at Markle. "Where are...?"

"Back," he said, in his more common clipped tone.

"Here," Morehouse said. He and Dana were approaching from the soup aisle, which is across from the cash register. "Nothing obvious. Markle, would you mind seeing if anything looks out of place?"

"You'll drive away business again," the store owner muttered, and led the two younger officers toward the back of the store.

What he said might not be exactly true, but I understood his thinking. The In-Town Market was robbed last fall. No one hurt and not much taken, but for a time patrons had stayed away.

Morehouse walked outside and Dana sat next to me. "The sergeant said something about you saw Joe in the store?"

I nodded. "I was in the back, looking at some coffee, and he walked out of the store room going to the front of the store."

"Did you talk to him?" Dana had pulled out a thin spiral notebook and I studied her for a few seconds as she uncapped a pen. Dana is roughly my age, and taller than my five foot two inches, but not much. She's pretty, but you don't notice her soft brown hair when it's pinned under her police hat.

"Just for a second. I told him I'd been to Java Jolt, and was glad he was all right."

"Did he respond?"

"Not directly. He just asked if anyone else was there and walked away. He said he had, I think he said *stuff* to do."

"Anything look odd? Did he seem stressed? Was he

carrying anything?"

"I saw him just for a second. He seemed preoccupied. Then he walked down the aisle next to mine to go out."

Dana turned toward Mr. Markle, who had returned to the front of the store. "When did Joe come in?"

"I didn't see him come in. He's not what you'd call chatty, but I order things for the coffee shop for him sometimes, so he talks to me more than to some."

Dana's head turned from right to left and settled back on Mr. Markle. "Security cameras?"

"No." He pointed to a larger round mirror that sat high on the wall near the ceiling. "Can't afford 'em. Keep my eyes on the mirrors, same as always. Have four of them."

She looked back at me. "I heard you said you think Joe got shot just around the corner on Seashore Street. Did you see anyone?"

"Not a soul."

Morehouse came back into the store and stood a few feet from me, frowning. "So, you talked to him?"

Dana went over what Mr. Markle and I had just said, in sort of police shorthand style.

"I was about to call you guys," I said to Morehouse. "Joe just seemed really odd, and I wasn't sure you knew where he was. That he was safe."

Morehouse snorted. "Safe."

I flushed and looked at him. "Will Joe be okay?"

"Not sure. He lost some blood. EMTs said he was semi-conscious when they loaded him. Where you gonna be today?"

His clipped tone annoyed me, but I knew him well enough not to press. "I'll go to the courthouse to look up some comps, and then to Harry's to write up the house I visited this morning."

"The courthouse'll have cops around. Harry's house locked up tight?"

"I didn't see anything when Joe got shot."

"Yeah, and a puppy thinks if he's under a rug you don't see him when he takes a leak."

As a uniformed officer sniggered and then moved away, I said, "I get what you're saying, but no one was near me. And I *didn't* see anything."

"Yeah, and I'm sure whoever it was is real sure of that and will leave you alone."

I STARED AT THE computer screen while the appraisal software loaded. Morehouse had instructed me to call him when I got to the office. I had done that, and for good measure checked to be sure all the doors and windows were locked on the first floor of Harry's former home.

A fly buzzed near the crown molding and then flew toward the window. The large office is to the right of the entry foyer, the living room on the left. Like Aunt Madge's, Harry's house is an older Victorian, with a large porch that he painted in several shades of green not long ago. Her house is larger and was better cared for through the years. She bought it about twenty-five years ago and converted it to a B&B, which she called the Cozy Corner. Because Harry had to replace a lot more fixtures and such, his front door is new and the windows are mostly double-paned. Not too many drafts.

My phone chirped and caller ID said it was Dr. Welby, a retired physician who serves on the Harvest for All Committee with me. I'm supposedly in charge, but he is a commanding presence with a lot of good ideas, so I'm happy to let him take the lead when he wants to. I figured he had heard I was near Joe's shooting and was calling to see if I was okay.

"Morning, Jolie. Say, didn't we talk about maybe some kind of fall canned drive or something?"

I guess he hasn't heard about Joe. "We did. Scoobie was just saying maybe we could do it as part of a Halloween party for kids. So many people with kids come to Harvest for All."

There were two beats of silence. Scoobie's fundraising ideas are sometimes off the wall. I could almost hear Dr. Welby assessing the extent to which a Halloween party could get out of hand.

Apparently he decided a party was safe. "That sounds doable. Do you have any ideas for a location?"

"How about we meet, um, soon to pick one? I bet Reverend Jamison or Father Teehan would let us use space at their churches."

"I might have another option. You free any evening?" he asked.

"Pretty much. Your calendar's busy. Why don't you check with the First Prez secretary and pick a date?"

"Will do. I'll get back to you later today or tomorrow."

I hung up, marveling that mundane life was so welcome after the morning I'd had. The software finished loading and I began entering the measurements of Mr. Fielding's house so the computer could draw a floor plan.

Living room, eleven by fourteen feet. *Where could the shooter have been standing?*

Hallway leading to kitchen, six feet by three feet. *Had to be around the corner on Seashore Street.*

Kitchen with breakfast area, fourteen by sixteen. *Joe walked toward me when he rounded the corner a few seconds after the shot. Had he been moving away from the person who shot him, or just coming back to the In-Town Market?*

Largest bedroom, eleven by thirteen feet, with small master bath, seven by six feet. *What could have caused Joe Regan to leave Java Jolt in such an apparent hurry?*

Middle bedroom, ten by twelve feet. *Was he deliberately walking toward me? What would he have had to say to me?*

Smallest bedroom, ten feet by eleven feet. *Who is the 'him' I'm supposed to not let get hurt?*

For some reason, I had given little thought to Joe's request. *It better not have been his dying request.*

I suddenly realized I had not told Morehouse what Joe had said to me. *How could you overlook that?* My forgetfulness could have hindered the police investigation. I swallowed some acidic saliva and blamed it on Mr. Markle's coffee.

"Nuts." I picked up the desk phone and dialed the non-emergency police number, wishing that I didn't have it memorized. The officer who answered said that Sergeant Morehouse would be with me in two minutes.

I knew nothing of Joe's private life. I bantered with him occasionally at Java Jolt, and he always donated something to Harvest for All when we had a fundraiser. Joe and Scoobie never seemed to get along too well, and our friend George has always butted heads with Joe. While that did not mean I'd been too reserved with Joe, I do trust Scoobie's judgment, so I hadn't gotten to know Joe well.

"What Jolie?" Morehouse's tone was brusque.

"Um, I forgot to tell you something." I paused.

"What the hell are you waiting for?"

"Joe said something to me."

It only took a few seconds to relay Joe's request, but longer for Morehouse to tell me what he thought about my memory lapse.

"I don't always see people bleeding on the sidewalk, you know."

He sighed. "Okay. You were shook. Anything else? You positive he didn't say who you were supposed to be sure didn't get hurt?"

"He definitely didn't say. Is he going to be able to talk to you?"

"You gonna keep this to yourself?" he asked.

"Sure."

"They stabilized him at Ocean Alley Hospital. Gave him a unit of blood. Then they moved him to Jersey Shore Hospital in Neptune for surgery."

"Surgery!"

"He had a bullet in the back, under one shoulder. Think it might have nicked a lung. Coulda been a lot worse."

I thought about Joe lying on his side, looking up at me. "Yes, I'm sure it could have. Thanks for telling me."

As soon as I hung up my mobile phone chirped. *Uh oh. Aunt Madge. I should have called her.*

She didn't even say hello. "Jolie, you didn't really get shot at this morning, did you?"

"No, Aunt Madge, but I did see Joe Regan soon after someone shot him." *Like three seconds soon.*

There were two beats of silence, and she must have passed the phone to Harry. "I was just leaving the house for the office. Were you at Mortimer Fielding's place? Are you okay? How is Joe?"

"I don't know much about Joe, but Sergeant Morehouse seemed to think the hospital was taking care of him. I'm fine. I was on the sidewalk on E Street, outside Mr. Markle's Market. It was just a coincidence that I was near Joe. And I had already been to the house."

"That wasn't my first concern," he said, in a dry tone.

In the background, Aunt Madge said, "When you see her be sure she's in one piece."

Harry said something to her quietly.

"But it will be Mr. Fielding's concern," I said. "He wants results before he decides on an asking price. With your favorite realtor, I might add."

"Just what I need," Harry said. "Maybe you should do something to make Lester angry at both of us."

I laughed. It felt good. "All we have to do is low-ball some appraisals and he'll go back to Stenner's." We wouldn't do it, of course, and I doubted my friend Jennifer Stenner, who inherited the larger appraisal business in town from her father, would want Lester's business. She knows he refers to her as "the Jennifer dame who charges too much for appraisals."

Harry said he would see me soon, and I had barely gone back to my computer screen when my phone chirped again.

"Did you honest to God get shot at?" George Winters gets excited easily.

"No. Who told you that? I was just nearby."

"Elmira Washington told Father Teehan and he called me to see if you were okay."

I suppressed a sigh. George and I dated briefly. It's annoying that people still expect him to know what I'm up to. "I'm surprised you aren't calling to give me a status update on Joe. You have lots of ins at the hospital."

"Joe who?"

"Geez. Sorry. Joe Regan."

"Joe got shot! You gotta be kidding."

I had momentarily forgotten that George had worked Saturday mornings at Java Jolt since the *Ocean Alley Press* fired him a few months ago. George is doing investigative work for an insurance company for a while, so he can qualify for a private detective license at some point. The pay at the insurance company isn't great.

It took less than a minute to tell George what happened. When I finished, he said, "I'm coming to Harry's," and hung up.

"Men," I muttered as I pressed the print button. "The men in my life know I can take care of myself, but they're always trying to ride to my rescue." An image of Harry on a horse came to mind, and I smiled.

I studied the printed floor plan for several minutes and noted where I had to give the computer different instructions. As I keyed in the changes that would put the kitchen on the right side of the house instead of the left, I thought more about what Joe had said.

I had no idea who he was talking about. Even in the off-season, dozens of people are in Java Jolt every day. Joe never mentioned family to me, though maybe he talked to George about that. Except they don't seem to do a lot of chit-chat, so probably not.

A key in the lock signaled Harry's arrival, and it was accompanied by a bark.

"Good. Mister Rogers." I stood to greet them. Harry's about five-nine. He has a reddish face and hair that has more white sprinkled in it than when I met him three years ago. He's in pretty good shape for a man in his seventies.

Harry shut the door and then let Mister Rogers off his leash. I bent down to pet the exuberant retriever. He, however, looked beyond me. "Are you looking for Jazz?" He and my small black cat sometimes have play dates at my bungalow.

"You look okay. I'm supposed to call Madge if you seem stressed." He gave me a peck on the cheek as Mr. Rogers headed for the kitchen in the back of the house.

"It'll catch up with me when I slow down. Joe spoke to me for a second, and I just talked to Morehouse about his condition." I paused.

Harry grinned and walked toward his desk. "Tell me and I won't tell George."

"Morehouse said Joe was stable."

"Good, good." Harry was distracted by seeing a page in the fax machine, which I had forgotten to check. He picked up the fax. "Lester wants us to call him before we give Mortimer Fielding the results."

"No surprise there." Someone knocked at the front door as I handed Harry the floor plan. "I loaded some pictures of the house in our photos folder."

George was visible through the door glass. He's almost six feet tall, and his dark auburn hair has a couple specks of grey. Not that I've heard him acknowledge this. Now that he works in an office rather than roams town snooping, George can't wear khaki shorts with a collared Hawaiian shirt. He wore tan casual slacks today, with a long-sleeved blue dress shirt that needed ironing. His blue and green tie was loosely knotted.

I let George in and he glanced across the foyer to the office Harry and I share. "Hey Harry, thanks for letting me barge in."

"No problem. Jolie, did you get comps?"

I guided George to the couch that sits in the living room and called over my shoulder. "Three good ones. I think they'll support the value I put in the computer."

"I can take a hint," George muttered.

"Harry's focused, not grumbling," I said. "What else did Elmira say?" Elmira Washington is one of those gossips who can have a mean edge to what she passes on. I don't like her.

"I think she really wanted to know what I'd heard. I didn't tell her she was the first person to tell me."

It was more than a gentle dig. As a former reporter, George thinks he should still be in the know about everything. Especially if it's something I know. "I had work to do, and Morehouse asked me not to talk much about it." Not exactly true, but true enough.

"Yeah, I'll let Tiffany bug Morehouse. He gets off easy with her." George frowned for a second, thinking of the reporter who replaced him at the *Ocean Alley Press*. "Did you see anything?"

"I heard two pops." I described Joe's look as he collapsed.

"Collapsed!"

"As in fell onto the sidewalk." I thought for a second. George could know who Joe was talking about. I lowered my voice. "He said something."

George leaned forward. "What?"

"Joe said, 'Don't let them hurt him.' Do you know who that could be? Someone who comes into Java Jolt?"

George frowned as he thought. "Hard to say. I don't think

of him as protective, except maybe for…"

"Max!" I nearly shouted.

"Damn," George said, but softly.

"What's wrong with Max?" Harry called.

Max is an Iraqi War vet who sustained a head injury that was serious enough to make him almost child-like. He repeats half of what he says in a staccato tone, and Joe gives him day-old muffins if Max comes by early in the morning.

Max could have been at Java Jolt early today.

CHAPTER THREE

I TOLD HARRY PROBABLY nothing was wrong with him, but George and I didn't want Max to hear about Joe's shooting from a stranger.

Harry walked to the door of our joint office as George and I got to the foyer. "Just give me the info on the comps and I'll start comparing them while you're gone."

Harry's slight frown told me he didn't like that I was leaving, but checking on Max had to be my priority. How else would I know he was safe?

We took my car, since George's insurance company employer provides his and it's not for personal use. I drove ten miles over the speed limit to get to Max's small bungalow, which he bought with his VA disability benefits.

Ocean Alley is not huge. It's less than two miles along the shore, and only twelve blocks deep. All of the north-south streets parallel the ocean and are named only with letters. While sometimes a lot of activity is packed into the relatively small area, it doesn't take more than ten or fifteen minutes to get anywhere.

We walked quickly up the short flight of steps at Max's house, and George knocked insistently. No response. I moved to the window that fronted the porch. The café curtains were not quite closed, so I peered through. Max's living room is a hodge-podge of hand-me-downs, but it's always neat. Nothing looked out of order.

"He could be anywhere," George said.

"He roams all day." My phone chirped. Scoobie's name was on the caller ID. Unlike George or Aunt Madge, he would not have expected an immediate call about Joe being shot. We were supposed to talk at lunch time. In case he was annoyed about not hearing from me, I'd say I would have called if I'd gotten hurt or something. Which I would have.

"Heard you've had a good morning," Scoobie said.

"Figured it would hold until lunch. I'm fine." A glance at my watch showed it was only eleven-ten. Scoobie's lunch hour started at noon.

"I have a visitor. And a boss who lets me take ad-hoc breaks."

The sound of a voice on a PA system told me Scoobie was at the hospital. I pushed the speaker phone button so George could hear him.

A voice apparently from behind Scoobie said, "Hi, Jolie. Jolie it's me, Max."

"Thank God he's with you, Scoobie. George and I are on Max's porch. I should have looked for him sooner."

"Good thing George is my best friend," Scoobie said. George rolled his eyes and Scoobie's teasing tone grew serious. "Max needs to talk to someone, and he won't let me call the police. I said if it turns out he needs to do that, you'd go with him."

"Of course. Meet you at the hospital cafeteria?" I asked.

"Mmm. Maybe the veranda, the one with picnic tables."

"Sure." Neither of us had to say that Max can be loud when he's excited, and a hospital cafeteria is not the place to yell about a shooting.

George and I walked down the steps. "Can I drive? I almost lost breakfast when you drove over here."

"No." I offered no explanation. What I thought was that I hadn't ridden in a car with George driving since we dated, and I didn't feel like having him remember the same thing. We're good as friends, but now and then he lets me know I was the one who ultimately broke off our relationship.

"Did you see Max anywhere near Java Jolt?" George asked.

"No, but I should have remembered about Joe giving him day-old muffins sometimes. Max could well have walked in on something."

"Hmm. I think I'll see what Tiffany knows." George pulled out his cell phone.

"I thought you mostly weren't talking to her."

"I decided to get over being ticked. It wasn't her fault the editor made a dumb-ass decision."

I smiled to myself. "In other words, you figured out that she can help you sometimes."

In my peripheral vision I saw George's grin. "Yeah. I've fed her a few story ideas. Keeps me on her good side...hey, Tiff." He paused, obviously listening. "Yeah, I think I know where she is. Can I check and call you right back?"

George ended the call as we pulled in front of the hospital. "She wants to talk to you. She'll tell us more if you do that."

I opened my car door and stepped out. "I can always hang up on her."

"Yeah, you're good at that." George pushed Tiffany's phone number again. "Yeah. Here she is...No, I didn't lie. I had no idea if Jolie would talk to you and I wanted to protect her privacy."

Tiffany's snort came through the phone as George handed his mobile to me.

"Hey Tiffany. Not a whole lot to tell if you already talked to the police."

Tiffany spoke fast in her usual high-pitched voice. "I know what I heard on the scanner, and I got there about a minute after the ambulance left." The frustration in her voice was evident. "Morehouse took my call for two seconds. He just said Joe was alive and, to quote him, 'might well live.' I'm hoping you know a little more."

Since it can be helpful to have a friend at the *Ocean Alley Press*, and not one who prints stupid pictures of me the way George did, I told her what I saw in front of the market. I didn't mention that Joe was in the In-Town Market's storage room. That seemed like Mr. Markle's business, and might not be something the police would want everyone knowing. I simply said I'd seen Joe in the store only long enough to exchange a greeting.

Tiffany sighed. "Not a lot more than I knew. Can I talk to George?"

George took his phone back. "Did you say thank you, Tiff?"

I couldn't hear her words as I walked toward the side of the three-story hospital, but it sounded as if Tiffany was growling. As we rounded the corner of the building, Scoobie and Max waved from one of the round, concrete picnic tables. I waved back.

George put his phone in his pants pocket. "The only thing she knows different is that the police are looking for a man who was running in the alley near the Java Jolt back door early this morning. Somebody other than Joe. Not much of a description except a white guy who ran fast. Dark clothes."

Max had risen and walked toward us. "Jolie, Jolie. I went to your house but you weren't there."

"What a smart thing to do," I said. Max is about five-seven, with dark brown hair and a thin physique. None of his war injuries show except for a very small scar on his left cheek, near his ear. I didn't even notice it when we first met. His head injuries had been severe, however, the result of riding in an Army vehicle that was not properly armored when it struck an explosive device at the side of the road.

Scoobie gestured to a spot next to him. "Have a seat, my love." I leaned over to kiss him and sat.

Max looked surprised, but it wasn't the time to discuss Scoobie's and my relationship. George sat and Max climbed onto the bench between George and me. "You okay?" I asked.

Max nodded, and studied his hands, which were now folded in front of him.

Scoobie's expression was more serious than usual. "Max went to the boardwalk to see Joe this morning."

"Muffins," Max said, "he gives me muffins."

"That's good," I murmured.

"And then what?" George asked.

Scoobie frowned at George. "As Max got closer to Java Jolt's back door, he heard Joe arguing with someone."

"They were really mad. Really mad," Max added.

"Did you hear why?" I asked.

"Something about Joe's name," he said. "Joe's name."

"Did, uh, the man dislike Joe's name?" I asked.

Max shook his head. "I don't know. He just said it was different. Different."

"Did he say how it was different?" George asked.

"No," Scoobie said. "Max said that Joe yelled at the man and asked him to leave."

"Told him," Max corrected. "Definitely told him."

"Right," Scoobie said, and looked at me. "Because the man was so angry, Max doesn't want to talk to the police."

Max continued to study his hands. "Sometimes they don't like me."

"They like you fine," I said, in a gentle tone. "When you were homeless they had to tell you not to sleep under the boardwalk."

"It was more than *that,*" Max emphasized the last word.

I laughed for a second. My smile faded as I realized that Max probably did not know Joe had been shot.

Scoobie kind of grunted a smile, and added, "You didn't cause trouble, Max. They aren't mad at you. How about if Jolie takes you to talk to Sergeant Morehouse or someone?"

He shook his head, firmly. "I walked away really fast. Fast. Someone yelled at me, but I was almost at the corner of the alley. I was fast."

This worried me. "Did someone see you, someone who was mad at Joe?"

"Only my back, my back. When I got to the end, I ran across the boardwalk and under it. Ran. They didn't know where I was." He finally lifted his gaze from his folded hands and looked at me. "Under the boardwalk."

"Did you see them?" George persisted.

Max stared at George, and it was not a friendly look. "No."

It occurred to me that while Max's mind had become childlike in some ways, his ability to sense danger had probably been honed pretty well in Iraq. Maybe he had seen someone well enough to identify them and didn't want to say so.

"Max, what if we go to my house and ask Sergeant Morehouse to come see you there?"

"Do you still have your pets?" he asked. "I like Jazz."

"I do." My black cat is friendly to Max, but her playmate usually stays under my bed.

"Ask the lady to come," he said. "Ask Dana."

I glanced at Scoobie before meeting Max's eyes again. "That will be Sergeant Morehouse's decision, but I bet he'll let Dana come."

WHEN WE GOT BACK to Steele Appraisals, a.k.a. Harry's house, George left in his own car and Max came inside with me. I needed to finish the paperwork for Mr. Fielding's house, since I had more or less promised him the results today. Then we could go to my house and call Morehouse to see if he'd let Corporal Dana Johnson talk to Max there.

"I like Harry," Max said, as I unlocked the front door.

"Me too, but I don't see his car, so he must be back at the Cozy Corner." *Max obviously doesn't know Joe was shot. How am I going to tell him that?*

Max trailed me into the shared office and I picked up a folder that was on the middle of Harry's desk. My name was prominently displayed on a paper attached to the folder.

"Jolie, this works. Because of the garage and the big shed in the back yard, we can probably even make Lester happy." I read the file. Harry had been extra helpful and added a paragraph about the house's attributes.

"Doubtful," I muttered. Max had walked across to the living room and was examining the one painting on the wall, a full-masted passenger ship from the mid-1800s. I picked up the phone to call Mr. Fielding. Lester might want a call first, but he wasn't paying for the appraisal.

Mortimer Fielding answered on the first ring. "Well, whaddya know?"

I gave him a one minute spiel about why his house was worth what Harry and I said it was. He made no response. "Mr. Fielding?"

"Lester said it's worth about eight thousand more."

"You can list it at any price you choose. Values are tricky now, because some people are skittish about buying at the shore. We base the appraised value on recent selling prices of houses like yours."

"Humph. You sound like you know what you're doin'."

Yea! "We're basically telling you what we believe the house is worth today. If you don't sell for six months, that number might go up, or down."

"You think down?"

"Predicting the real estate market is more Lester's area of expertise." As if anyone can reliably predict housing values after Hurricane Sandy.

I said I would drop a copy of the printed appraisal at his house, and he said later today or early tomorrow was all right. Pleased at the lack of argument, I made a copy on our small office copier, stuck it in a separate manila folder, and placed it in the filing cabinet.

I shut the cabinet drawer and walked out of the office area to look down the hall to the kitchen, where Max had wandered. "Max, before we ask Sergeant Morehouse to come to my house to talk to you, we need to chat for a minute."

He walked toward me. "I want to talk to Dana."

"I expect that will be fine, but I don't know if she's working this afternoon." I pointed to the couch, the only piece of furniture in the living room. "Have a seat."

Max stared at me. "Why sitting, Jolie? Sitting."

"We don't have to sit. I just wanted to make sure you knew that Joe is fine."

"Joe yelled. Yelled."

"Yes, he did. And then I think he went for a walk." I was trying to gauge what Max knew, and decided nothing more than he had relayed at the hospital.

"Walking. I walk. A lot."

I smiled. "Joe's okay, but when he was walking, someone tried to hurt him."

Max's mouth formed an o. "Sitting is good." He stared at me as he sat, and I sat next to him, about one foot away.

"I saw Joe at Mr. Markle's store, after you saw him."

Max's expression cleared. "Mr. Markle likes me now."

"Yes. When Joe walked out of the store, someone, I don't know who, tried to shoot him, and..."

Max sat up straighter. "Was it enemy fire?"

"Um, not like you experienced in Iraq. All they did was hit him in the shoulder. He's going to be fine."

Max stood. "I need to go to the bathroom. The bathroom." He walked toward the kitchen, and I figured he had noticed the half-bath earlier.

I stayed seated and worried. I shouldn't have told him when we were by ourselves. Maybe we should have gone over to First Prez, to see Reverend Jamison.

The toilet flushed. I stood, prepared to comfort Max. However, he walked back into the living room and said, "Mr. Markle sells donuts."

I guess the discussion is over. "Maybe we can go there later. Are you ready to go to my house, Max?"

"I was always ready."

I smiled. "I know. Thanks for waiting."

I locked the office as we left, and waited a few seconds on the short sidewalk that led to the street. Max had to check out a huge chrysanthemum plant that looked more like a red bush. "I have milk and orange juice at home. You want anything else to drink?"

"Scoobie lives with you. He didn't move back to his old apartment after it got fixed. Didn't move back."

"That's true." I unlocked the passenger door for him. "Scoobie can explain that to you."

I walked behind my car and had just turned right to walk toward the driver's door when the screech of tires and sound of a roaring engine made me jump, and turn. A very large, dark green SUV barreled toward me.

CHAPTER FOUR

I HEARD MY CAR'S passenger door open and sensed Max behind me. He slid across the trunk on his stomach, grabbed my collar and then upper arms, and pulled me across the trunk. We landed in a heap on the grass by the curb. The SUV swerved and hit my back passenger door with the sound of metal grating on metal. A very loud sound.

The whole thing didn't take much more than five seconds. Max disentangled himself quickly and stood. He took a few steps as if he planned to give chase, and then stopped to stare after the car. It was at the end of the block and screeching around the corner in a flash.

My elbow was sore but not broken, and my neck was stiff from being pulled so hard across the trunk. But I was alive and very grateful to be.

I rolled on my side and then stood. "Max! You're okay, right?"

He faced me, his brown eyes dull. "I got out of the way that time."

NEIGHBORS MUST HAVE CALLED the police, because sirens wailed before Max and I were back in the house. Within three minutes, a young responding officer was in

Harry's living room. He calmly called in a description of the vehicle and the direction it was headed. Not that I could tell him much. I hadn't seen a license plate. Max had not spoken since we got in the house.

Harry had arrived within five minutes of my phone call to him. Aunt Madge had bread in the oven for her guests' afternoon tea and hadn't accompanied him. It's also possible she's getting more laid back about what she has called my escapades.

Harry and I sat next to Max on the couch. The officer, I thought his name was Leland, keyed something into a hand-held computer.

"Max, did I thank you?" I asked.

He looked up from where he had been staring at the floor. "About twelve times. Maybe ten. More than ten."

"May I give you a small hug?"

He looked surprised. "I give hugs."

I leaned toward him and did a quick, one-armed hug around his shoulders and pulled back. "I may need to say thank you another day."

Footsteps on the porch made us look toward the front door. Sergeant Morehouse and Dana Johnson walked in.

Morehouse gave full meaning to the word sputter. "Jolie, what the hell happened now?"

I stood to look him in the eyes. "You tell me. All I do is appraise houses. If Max hadn't been with me I'd have been crushed."

"Good for you, Max," Dana said. Max kept staring at the floor.

"Sit," Morehouse said, looking at me and pointing to the couch.

"Shall I bark?" He reddened slightly and I said to Dana, "There are extra chairs in the office."

"Tell me what happened. All of it," Morehouse said. He sat next to me on the couch, and turned so he could face me.

"It starts, I think, with this morning." I told him that I'd realized Max might have seen something at Java Jolt, described how George and I looked at his house before we heard from Scoobie, and ended by recounting how Max had saved me from the speeding car.

Dana had dragged a wooden chair from Harry's office, one that's used on the rare occasion a client comes to see us. She placed it across from Max.

"Good for you, Max." Morehouse said this as he looked from me to Max and back to me. He had toned down his irritation, but I knew that was largely because of Max.

"So Max," Dana said, with a slight smile, "I didn't know you could lift something as heavy as Jolie."

"She's not too heavy. I learned in physical therapy. Before that in the Army. The Army. But before I went to Iraq, not…there."

None of us knew much about Max's past. His friend Josh used to be more like a caregiver, but as Max has gotten to know more people in Ocean Alley he's better able to fend for himself.

"It's a good thing you still know how to move fast," Dana said.

Even Morehouse seemed to recognize that Dana was trying to put Max at ease, so he let her continue.

"I bet you went to Joe's to get some muffins this morning."

At this Max smiled for the first time since we met at the hospital. "They're good. Good." He frowned. "But I couldn't smell cooking. It was still sort of dark, but Joe had a flashlight. A flashlight."

"Those are good to have," Dana continued. "Did you see the light moving in Java Jolt?"

"Yes, but only in the back, the back. Through the window."

"There's a window in the back door," I said, and Dana nodded.

"So, Max, you saw the light moving around."

He nodded.

"Did you see it in Joe's hand, or could someone else have been holding it?"

Morehouse tapped a pencil on his notebook, but said nothing. I could tell he wanted Dana's questions to move faster.

"I, uh," Max looked panicked. "I don't know."

Harry spoke from where he leaned against the wall near the couch. "That's not a wrong answer, Max, it just helps Dana to know."

"Oh, okay." He thought for a few seconds. "I guess I just thought it was Joe. Joe."

"I would have thought that, too," Dana said. Now, let's go over what you heard."

Max repeated what he had said to Scoobie, George, and me at the hospital. He added one thing. "The other man talked different."

"Can you say how it was different?" Morehouse asked.

"Do you know the Golden Girls?" Max asked.

Dana looked flummoxed, but Morehouse said, "The TV show? With the lady roommates?"

Max nodded. "He talked like Blanche."

Morehouse turned to Dana. "TV show in repeats, on a lot after midnight. Blanche has a southern accent."

I tried a line with a southern dialect. "So, Maaax," I drew out his name, "do you like white rah-ice?"

Max stared at me. "Kind of like that. But louder. I like brown rice, brown."

"Me too," Dana said.

"Blanche's dresses are the nicest," he added. "Nicest."

"I think so, too," Morehouse said. "If we showed you some pictures, do you think you would recognize the…"

Max shook his head several times. "I didn't look. I ran. Just ran."

"What made you run?" I asked, as Morehouse scowled at me.

"The man was mad at Joe. He said Joe was…a bunch of bad names. Bad names."

"Can you tell us which ones?" Dana asked.

Another firm headshake. When Dana kept looking at him, he said. "One started like shush."

"Ah, I get it," Dana said. She turned to Morehouse. "Anything else you want to ask?"

I smirked for only a second, but Morehouse saw it. I'd never heard Dana take over questioning before. I liked her style.

"No, Corporal, thanks. So, Max, how about if Dana drives you home?"

"The police aren't a taxi service." Max almost parroted this. This was probably the response when he'd asked for a ride in the past.

Morehouse smiled. "That's right. But I want Dana to make sure your house is safe"

"I'm staying with Scoobie." Max said this with a trace of stubbornness.

Morehouse looked at me and I shrugged.

"Okay, but let's have Dana check and you can pick up a change of clothes."

Max looked at Dana. "Jazz likes cat treats."

She stood and grinned. "Jolie can tell Scoobie to bring some home."

After making sure I was going to be okay, Harry said he'd leave with Dana and Max so he could let Aunt Madge know I was in one piece.

A sort of metallic grating sound came in as the three walked out. I stood to look out the window. A tow truck had my car on a winch. I sighed and turned back to Morehouse. "A lot of damage, you think?"

"Do I look like a mechanic?"

"Not especially. Now what?"

"When were you going to have Max talk to me?"

"We were on our way to my house, to ask you to send Dana over there. Max didn't want to go to the station. I just needed to stop here to pick up a file."

He fumed. "Wrong priority. This is why amateurs should have nothing to do with police investigations."

"On the other hand," I smiled as sweetly as I could, "people do talk to me even if they avoid you."

SCOOBIE AND I watched Max take a third helping of mashed potatoes. The three of us were at the small dinette table in the living-dining room of my bungalow. Now Scoobie's and my bungalow. There's not a lot of room for two of us in the nine-hundred square foot house, but at least there is a second bedroom.

Scoobie's eyes met mine. "Good you learned to make mashed potatoes."

"They need more milk," Max said, and Scoobie hid a smile behind his hand.

"Thanks, Max, I've never been a very good cook."

He stopped eating and looked at me. "Couldn't Aunt Madge teach you?"

Aunt Madge is well known for her muffins, which she can make in any flavor. Except prunes. Her dogs like them, so she no longer buys prunes.

"Jolie would have to sit still long enough to listen," Scoobie said.

"You're oh so funny." I stood. "I think I'm going to read for a few minutes while you and Max wash the dishes." I smiled at Max, and walked toward the bedroom Scoobie and I share.

Max called after me. "I'm a very good cleaner."

I propped two pillows behind my head and stretched out on the bed. The book on my stomach was mostly a prop.

We didn't know more about Joe's condition except that he was out of surgery at Jersey Shore Hospital and doctors had removed a bullet and repaired what turned out to be a collapsed lung. The bullet had not made a full puncture in it, fortunately. We wouldn't even have known that if Aunt Madge hadn't volunteered at Ocean Alley Hospital years ago. She had, of course, headed the hospital auxiliary for a couple of years and knows people everywhere.

What did the angry man mean about a different name? And why would whoever was in Java Jolt be mad enough at me to try to run me over?

I could probably answer the second question. If someone had noticed me at Java Jolt soon after Joe left, perhaps they thought I had seen them arguing. The boardwalk looked empty, but I hadn't searched between the buildings before entering Java Jolt. Nor had I paid attention to who was on the boardwalk when I left.

If I get smashed I can't talk about anything I saw.

Scoobie and Max were in the hallway that opened to each of the two bedrooms and the bathroom. Scoobie told Max where towels and such were.

Other than my concern for Max I did not have what my father would call a pony in this race.

Unless someone had seen me and thought I had or knew about something they wanted. What could that be? Maybe I should ask Joe why someone would run him out of Java Jolt and then shoot him. Perhaps I could call…

"Damn." I sat up. I hadn't called my sister. She lives thirty miles inland in Lakewood, the town I called home until my ex-husband poured a lot of our money and some of his employer's into casino coffers.

My sister, Renée, and I have a deal. If I can't manage to stay out of the papers, and if I call her, she'll run interference for me with our parents. Thankfully they retired to Florida a few years ago. For some reason, I tend to push my mother's buttons. Renée, who is six years older than I am, seems to have a knack for not doing that.

I went to the desk that's wedged into a corner of the bedroom and turned on my laptop. Email was better. No recriminations. At least not verbal ones.

Uh oh. An email from Renée.

"So, you're up to hijinks? Aunt Madge called. Lucky for

you most of Mom and Dad's friends moved away, too. Let me know if you need to borrow a car."

And that was it. *She's learned how to chill.*

I sent Renée a response that said all I really did was see Joe after he was shot, and the swipe at my car could have been an accident. *Yeah, right.* I added that I thought my insurance would pay for a rental car.

I shut the computer and went back to my thinking position on the bed. The door opened and Scoobie stood in the doorframe. "And as usual, you were just in the wrong place at the wrong time." His frown was mostly fake.

I patted the bed next to me. Scoobie was in his non-work uniform of blue jeans and a Harvest for All tee shirt. He untied his sneakers and lay down next to me. I reached for his hand, and we both stared at the ceiling for a moment.

He looked at me. "Anything I need to know besides what you and Max said you told the police?"

I shook my head, slowly. "It's hard to convey how distracted Joe looked when he came out of Mr. Markle's storage room. I mean, I told him I'd been at Java Jolt. He knew it was open and untended, but he barely paused."

"It is odd." Scoobie reached toward the table that held an alarm clock, lamp and a small pad of paper and pen. He passed the paper and pen to me. "This is usually when you start one of your lists."

"You may know me too well."

"True. I would really like it if that list said things like how to be sure no one mad at Joe knows where I live."

"The only thing I really care about is Max. We've got to be sure no one can hurt him."

"Jolie."

Scoobie's expression seemed half-amused, half-frustrated. "I never mind helping Max, but if he's really in danger the police need to pay more attention to him."

"I know, but we can, too." I squeezed Scoobie's hand. At times he and I see things differently, especially when it comes to figuring out something that I think doesn't add up. I love the guy to pieces and always consider what he thinks. But not always as much as he might like.

CHAPTER FIVE

NOT LONG AFTER SCOOBIE left for work the next morning Max said he needed to go. I had heard him tell Scoobie the futon in the guest room was not comfortable, and I expected him to say he was going home. However, when I asked him his plans for the day, Max said that he visited Mr. Markle each day when the store opened.

"You want me to drive you?" I asked.

Max stared at me.

"What?"

Max smiled. "Sergeant Morehouse drove you here. Your car is smashed. Very smashed."

Damn. "Your memory is better than mine."

His smile faded. "Only today."

"You can stay here tonight, you know."

Despite what I heard him tell Scoobie earlier, he seemed to consider this. "Jazz slept with me. Right next to me."

"So, you'll come back later?"

Max shook his head. "Can I look under your bed?"

"Sure. Pebbles likes you, she's just shy."

Max, followed by Jazz, walked into the room Scoobie and I share, and knelt to look at my pet skunk. Not everyone has one of those. It had been my luck to inherit the one that had belonged to the house's prior owner, a widow who died about eighteen months ago. Fortunately, Pebbles' scent glands had been removed. Even so, her presence probably cuts down on the number of people who would otherwise drop in unannounced.

Jazz walked under the bed and Max scratched the carpet at the edge of the bed, presumably to encourage Pebbles to come out. She did not.

"If you sit on the couch for a while she'll forget you're here and wander out to use her litter box," I said.

Max stood quickly. "I don't want to bother her. Bother her."

Max declined my offer to make him breakfast. I reminded him that he could not get muffins at Java Jolt, and he said Arnie, who owns the popular Newhart's Diner in town, lets him order only one pancake and water.

"I have to go out for a while, but you can stop by the Cozy Corner and see Aunt Madge if you get lonely later."

"I know everyone. I'm never lonely." He put on the lightweight brown windbreaker that he'd worn yesterday. "I could go visit Aunt Madge's dogs, though. Her dogs."

Max left. Before I called Aunt Madge I wanted to read the paper.

Java Jolt Owner Shot

Joe Regan, who owns the Java Jolt Coffee Shop on Ocean Alley's boardwalk, was shot on Seashore Street near the corner of E and Seashore. He collapsed on E Street. Regan was taken first to Ocean Alley Hospital and later transferred to a larger hospital. His condition was unknown at press time, but he was reported to have spoken soon after being wounded.

This was not Regan's first problem of the day. At about 6:45 A.M., a customer entered the shop and found it vacant. The customer, real estate appraiser Jolie Gentil, said she found the front and back doors unlocked and Regan's bank deposit bag on the floor near the back door.

Investigating officers found no sign of Regan between 6:45 and when he was shot at about 8:25 A.M. Just before the shooting, Regan visited another downtown business, but he had no substantive conversation with anyone.

Because police have not been able to interview Regan they cannot say whether anything was stolen from Java Jolt. A small amount of money in the cash register was not taken. Java Jolt is closed until further notice.

That's not too bad. Not great for Joe or his business, but at least it wasn't his obituary. I turned the page and groaned at the site of another article.

SUV Appears to Target Resident

Ferry Street was nearly the site of a hit-and-run yesterday afternoon, when Jolie Gentil was barely able to jump out of the way of a speeding SUV.

Gentil told police that she was behind her car, walking toward the driver's side door, when a dark-colored SUV pulled out of a nearby parking space and came toward her. Neither Gentil nor a companion was able to get the vehicle's license tag number.

Sergeant Morehouse of the Ocean Alley Police said the department would like residents to call if they saw a black or dark green speeding, late model SUV at about one PM yesterday afternoon near the vicinity of G and Ferry Streets.

The article provided the public police department phone number but, mercifully, not Max's name. Had it been any other adult, the *Press* would have identified him. I assumed police had asked the paper not to publicize Max's involvement, since he would be considered vulnerable to anyone who thought Max might be able to identify them.

That concept hadn't kept the *Press* from using my name. I picked up the phone and called the paper. When Tiffany came on the line I tried to keep my tone neutral. "Tiffany, are you trying to tell a prospective murderer how to find me?"

"What do...oh, you mean your name? I can't leave a name out unless the police tell me."

"You left Max's out."

"Well, yeah," she stammered, "but you're not, like, disabled."

I took a breath. "I'm not. But I'm in and out of vacant houses, and I don't own a crash helmet." Tiffany started to say something, but I interrupted. "Just tell your editor I'll ask him to pay hospital bills if someone comes after me again." I hung up. *That went well. Not.*

It took me thirty seconds to calm down. If the SUV

attack, which was how I was beginning to think of it, was the only major event yesterday and police believed it to be an accident, I might understand using my name. But since I saw Joe just after he was shot? The first article not only named me, but said I was a real estate appraiser. It was like leaving bread crumbs to my location.

What did the SUV driver think I knew or had seen?

Now that I knew what Aunt Madge would have read in the paper, I called her.

"I was going to call you in a bit," she said. "I thought you might sleep in today."

"Scoobie gets up early, and Max stayed here last night."

"That's good. Were the people in that car yesterday after Max, do you think?"

"It's hard to know." I chose my words carefully. If I told her I thought Max was in danger, she would infer I was. "I don't know if they were really aiming for anyone. Max didn't see who hurt Joe, and I certainly didn't. I think whoever shot him would know that."

"Scuttlebutt has it that Max may have seen someone with Joe early yesterday morning, well before the shooting."

For someone who hates gossip, she hears everything. "He says he didn't, but I suppose the driver might think he did. Max didn't want to hang around here. He said he might stop by to see you and the dogs."

"Glad you told me. I have to go out once or twice, but I'll leave a note and tell him to sit on the porch." Her tone changed to sound less social and more serious. "Even if that car was aiming for you, it's not your job to find the driver. Leave it to the police."

"Yes, ma'am." *I might try to figure out who was so angry*

with Joe. That's not exactly looking for the driver.

"You're being coy."

"I promise not to look for the car's driver."

"Good. Call Renée later." Aunt Madge said good bye and hung up.

I felt a bit irritated. I never look for trouble, and I'm thirty-one, not twelve. *People should trust my judgment more.*

THE RENTAL CAR office is just off the lobby of the town's oldest and largest hotel, Beachcomber's Alley. Unfortunately, the hotel is almost half a mile from my bungalow. Since I didn't want to bother Aunt Madge I set out, reminding myself that some of the buildings on my college campus were almost that far apart.

Not too many people rent cars in Ocean Alley, so the woman who rents the cars, Ginger Perkins, also works part-time at the hotel front desk. I waited while she checked out a hotel guest who thought the towels should be larger.

A notepad with the hotel's logo was on the small table I sat next to, so I helped myself to a sheet and started a to-do list.

1. Call hospital about Joe.
2. Call Renée for sure
3. Visit Joe?
4. Call Lester about Mortimer Fielding

Ginger, loose-flowing brown curls bouncing on her shoulders, walked from the hotel counter to the alcove that housed the rental car desk. "I thought I'd see you today, Jolie."

Gotta love small towns.

"Yep. If I'm going to walk it'll be for exercise." *Which I need to do more of. My jeans are tight.*

Ginger opened a notebook and frowned slightly. "I only have two cars, and I don't know if your insurance will cover the full rental on them. They're bigger and rent for more than most companies pay for accident rentals."

"Swell. I called them this morning. I can call them back."

After ten minutes of phone conversation with my agent, during which time Ginger checked out a guy who sported a blue spiked Mohawk, my agent agreed to pay the higher price, with the proviso that Ginger would get me switched to a smaller model when she had one available.

At least whoever's mad at Joe wouldn't know what I was driving.

RENTAL CAR AT THE READY, I called Jersey Shore Hospital in Neptune. The operator said there was no patient named Joe Regan. I decided not to believe her, and drove to Neptune, which is only about eight miles from Ocean Alley.

The two towns have little in common. Where Ocean Alley has twenty thousand residents after September and no buildings higher than four stories, Neptune has about twenty-eight thousand people and could be a town in any state. Several eight or ten story buildings are spread through the town, and life does not revolve around the ocean and the tourists it brings.

The hospital was a lot newer than Ocean Alley's, which was built in the 1950s. I walked by the information desk, having decided that if the hospital didn't acknowledge Joe was a patient, I couldn't ask for him. If I did, it might also alert hospital security that a gunshot victim had an unexpected visitor.

The elevator was just off the lobby. A glance at a sign next to it indicated patients were on floors three to five. That would mean a lot of wandering around peering into rooms.

Before getting on the elevator I followed signs that directed people to the hospital gift shop. I had no plans to buy helium-filled balloons or a large vase of flowers, but wanted to carry something that indicated I was going to visit a patient. A coffee mug filled with lollipops seemed appropriate, so I paid for that and a card that was blank inside.

What do you say to a gunshot victim? *How are the holes healing?*

I decided just to say that "all of us" (whoever that would be) looked forward to his return to Ocean Alley and Java Jolt. A dose of paranoia made me sign with just a J.

I boarded the elevator, pressed the fifth floor button, and studied a framed sign on the elevator wall that gave specific information on what was on each floor.

The Intensive Care Unit was on three, which was the same floor as the operating rooms. If Joe was in ICU I'd never get to see him. Given how quickly patients are moved out of ICU these days, I thought he might be on a regular patient floor or in the Step-Down Unit. That was for people who needed less attention than ICU but more than somebody who'd had a routine operation.

The Step-Down rooms were on the fourth floor. When I got to the fifth floor, a nurse got on the elevator. I pressed four and she pressed Lobby. The elevator opened to a fourth-floor hallway that offered two choices. Step Down was on the left and General Medical/Surgery was on the right. I decided to go to the right. It was nine-thirty; maybe a nursing assistant would be walking Joe down the hall.

No such luck. It was probably too soon after surgery for him to be out in the hall. I finished a leisurely stroll through the Med/Surg wing, as I'd heard Scoobie call it, and walked past the elevator into the Step-Down Unit.

Computers the nurses used to record patient status sat on carts with wheels; it looked like one for about every three or four patients. No patients were in the hall, but as I walked to the end of the hallway and turned left, a group of people in scrubs and white lab-jacket type clothes came out of a room and walked quickly ahead of me. "The next one," said an officious looking man with a bald head and very straight spine," is recovering from a gunshot wound that collapsed his left lung. He also has a broken left..."

The group, which I gathered was doing some kind of hospital rounds, walked into a room on my right. I kept going. When I got to a small waiting area at the end of the hall I sat down and placed the coffee mug, now minus an orange lollipop, on a table next to me.

There could be other patients getting over a collapsed lung, but not likely another who had gotten it from a gun. *Could I really be this lucky?*

I had half-expected to see a police officer at the door to Joe's room. If he was not listed under his own name, maybe the police thought he'd be safe. Not that Joe had to worry about me, but what about someone else?

I leafed through a local magazine, wishing I could do as it proclaimed possible and make room dividers from driftwood. I had a second lollipop in my mouth when the entourage of medical staff walked by. They were talking quietly, and the only words I picked up on were "full recovery." I hoped they were talking about Joe.

After another minute, I put down my magazine, retrieved my purse and the coffee mug of lollipops, and made my way toward the room I thought was Joe's. I walked slowly by the door. When I heard no voices, I turned and went back a few paces and into the room.

Like rooms in most newer hospitals, it was a single that had a privacy curtain around the bed. I walked quickly to the far side of the room and stood between the curtain and the window, wondering if I should peek in.

I whispered, "Joe?"

Nothing.

"Joe?"

"Mmm?"

I tugged on one end of the curtain and pulled it back a few inches so I could peer in.

Joe was very white, a fact made more apparent by his auburn hair. A tube went from his chest to a hidden container of some kind on the other side of the bed. An IV line was in his right arm and an oxygen cannula graced his face, but there was no other paraphernalia. He had a cast on his left arm, which was in a sling and slung across his chest. The fingers that stuck out of the cast were swollen. He had probably broken the arm when he fell after he was shot.

Joe looked at me and closed his eyes. He mumbled what sounded like, "Shoulda known." Then his eyes opened wide and he stared at me. In barely more than a whisper, he asked, "Max?"

I spoke as quietly. "He's fine. He found Scoobie at the hospital, and then he stayed with us last night."

Joe's face relaxed, but his expression looked as if he had

questions he was too tired to ask.

I tried to think of what he wanted to know. "Max doesn't think anyone saw more than his back when he ran away."

Joe shook his head lightly. I wasn't sure what that meant, but figured I could come back to it. "Do you know who shot you?"

For a second his expression seemed cagey, then it cleared, and he whispered, "Accident."

"Baloney." I said this in an almost normal tone of voice, and paused to see if anyone had heard me. The coffee mug was still in my hand and I placed it on the rolling table that sits by all hospital beds.

Joe had a trace of a smile, but as I reached for the card in my purse, the smile vanished. We both heard a loud voice in the hall, maybe a couple of doors down from Joe's room.

"Sposed to be near the nurses' station so they can keep an eye on him."

Morehouse!

Feeling panicked, I moved outside the curtain and turned a full 360 degrees. A tiny closet was on the wall opposite Joe's bed. Without pausing, I opened it and almost dove in, then turned so I faced the now-closed closet door.

My heart was beating so hard it seemed anyone within ten feet would hear it. Footsteps came into the room and someone pulled aside the curtain that surrounded Joe's bed.

Morehouse's tone was almost kindly. "You look better than I thought you would."

Joe didn't say anything, but he must have acknowledged Morehouse in some way, because the sergeant continued, "Don't want to badger you, but I'm hopin' you can give us an idea of who did this to you."

When Joe didn't say anything, Morehouse added, "Don't want anyone else to get hurt, especially Max, or everyone's favorite busybody, Jolie."

I could hear Joe's sheets rustle, and it sounded as if he whispered something.

"Max is okay," Morehouse said. "I saw him yesterday. Max said he was comin' to see you to get some muffins, real early yesterday, and he heard someone arguing with you. He hasn't really said if he heard anything specific, except a lot of swear words he don't want to repeat."

Finally Dana spoke. I had hoped what sounded like a second set of footsteps entering the room was hers. "We'll keep an eye on him, and let some of the other business owners know to call us if it looks as if a stranger is bothering him. Or maybe it's not a stranger?"

Dana's question invited a response, but Joe did not seem to have one.

"Thing is," Morehouse continued, "we lifted prints from your shop. Lots of 'em, of course. But one set on the back door came up when we ran it. A guy from a not-so-big town in Kansas. Just got out of the slammer after doin' a three-year sentence for bank robbery. Armed robbery, but first offense and he didn't use the weapon. He mighta had a partner, but he wouldn't say."

Plastic tore and I figured Morehouse had unwrapped a lollipop. I felt angry at Morehouse's insinuation. Grouchy as Joe could be sometimes, the idea of him being in cahoots with a bank robber seemed far-fetched.

Why question Joe about a crime from a few years ago-- especially when Joe was so very badly injured? Unless Joe really was a partner in a bank robbery. Joe was in Rotary, for heaven's sake. He sold coffee at Harvest for All fundraisers and gave us the profits. *But Joe didn't ask the robber's name.*

Morehouse continued. "I'm not sayin' you know the guy." *Yes you are.*

"Just wonderin' if you know anyone like that. Or anything."

Joe's voice was a rasp I could barely hear. "Lived in Kansas. Didn't know," he paused to take a breath, "any thieves."

"Glad you mentioned you used to live there."

I inferred Morehouse was saying that if Joe had not said he had lived there it would mean Morehouse thought Joe was holding back something important. *When did Joe live in Kansas?*

"Lemme tell you the description we heard."

I could hear Morehouse turn pages in the notebook he always carries, but it was Dana who spoke. "Max didn't have a description. He thought the man arguing with you had a Southern accent. But because someone was running down the boardwalk fast at that time of the morning, a guy attracted attention. After word got around that you were hurt, a couple folks called. Man was maybe five ten, white, no idea of hair color because he had on a ball cap. Had on blue jeans and a dark-colored, long-sleeved shirt."

"Had back door open, for light." Joe cleared his throat and paused for several seconds. "Guy came in, wanted my deposit money." He sounded as if he needed to cough.

"Did he get it?" Morehouse asked.

The bang of a door hitting the wall almost made me jump out of the closet.

"Who are you?" The woman's tone was authoritative.

Sergeant Morehouse spoke. "This is Corporal Dana John..."

"This man is much too sick for an interview. You have to leave *right now.*"

"Just anoth..." Morehouse began.

"Now, or I call hospital security."

Dana said, "Thanks," and Morehouse muttered, "Later Joe."

They left and the nurse's shoes squeaked as she moved on the tile floor to be close to Joe. "I'm sorry, Mr. Smith. I have three patients here in Step-Down, and one of them needed more of my attention for a few minutes."

The sound of Joe's bed being moved up--or down--reached me. The nurse added, "Your call button is right here. If anyone else tries to make you talk, just press it. Do you need anything?"

Joe must not have answered, because she started for the door. "We'll keep this mostly closed so you can get some rest."

I waited almost a full minute and then opened the closet door. I walked close to Joe's bed and peered around the curtain. The nurse had raised the head of his bed a few inches.

Joe's gaze fell on me and he shook his head very slightly.

"I'll leave you alone, too," I said, softly. "I just wanted you to know Max was okay and we're all pulling for you."

That wasn't totally true, I wanted to know more. But I had to accept that I couldn't ask him now. I took the card out of my purse and laid it next to the coffee mug of lollipops. *Thank goodness the card wasn't out when Morehouse was here.*

CHAPTER SIX

ON THE DRIVE BACK to Ocean Alley I thought about what I'd learned. I had never known Joe once lived in Kansas, but why would I? Morehouse had not named the town, but how many armed robberies had there been in Kansas maybe four or five years ago? Armed robberies where police thought there could be an accomplice but the robber wouldn't name him? And why wouldn't the guy who went to prison name his accomplice? On television that was the kind of bargaining chip that got criminals reduced sentences.

I thought about how people described the man who was seemingly running away from Java Jolt. The description was no help, and it was more puzzling why someone had left at a run. Joe's visitor was the aggressor. Did Joe do something to force the man to leave? Joe is very fit. I've always thought he had a lifeguard's physique. He could have rousted the man in some way. Or maybe the man saw Max looking in and went after him.

You should stay out of this. That would be Scoobie's advice. I trust his judgment, but he wasn't the one who was almost run over by an SUV.

My thoughts turned back to Max. He had become independent in so many ways, but his thinking was far from that of an adult, and he was alone much of the time. I was about to turn onto Ferry from G Street to go to the appraisal office when I had an idea.

Max loves to help distribute food at Harvest for All, which we do three days each week. I don't usually encourage him to help, because his enthusiasm can slow us down. However, if I put him on the food pantry volunteer schedule for a week or two, I'd know to look for him if he didn't show up.

Now what? I stopped at Burger King for an early lunch and was greeted by a holler from Lester Argrow. He usually walked from his small office above First Bank, so he had no car parked in the Burger King lot. No way to avoid him, in other words.

"Jolie! Get your grub and come over here." Lester gestured from a table in a far corner of the eatery.

I gave Lester my practiced four-finger wave and ordered a burger and Dr. Pepper. He would want to badger me about the appraisal for Mr. Fielding's house if the figures seemed low to him. I didn't feel up for a badgering, but he does send Steele Appraisals more business than any other realtor.

I slid into the booth across from him as Lester closed the *Ocean Alley Press* and pushed aside the remnants of an order of french fries. "So, kid, guess you got it right on the Fielding place. At least old Mortimer thinks so."

I unwrapped my burger. "Harry and I worked hard to give him an estimate that will help you and him price it to sell."

"You know, if it wasn't for the damn comp thingys I could list 'em higher."

"List maybe, but perhaps not sell." I raised my Dr. Pepper as if toasting him.

Lester can change tacks faster than a sailboat in the

America's Cup race. "So, whaddya think about how Joe got shot? You bein' there, and all."

"I was around the corner." Before he could ask another question I added my own. "Did you hear anybody say who they thought did it?"

He shook his head. "Couple other realtors think maybe a thief figured Joe's burglar alarm was off because of the storm. Everybody knows he takes his deposit to the bank in the morning. Means there's money there overnight. Maybe Joe was walking to the bank."

"Hmm. That sounds like someone who knows him."

Lester shrugged. "Yeah, or somebody who watches who goes in and out of the bank when."

"It doesn't make sense he'd do it in the morning. He opens early. The bank doesn't."

"You heard of ATMs, right?"

I ignored the question. "He doesn't always have a helper, especially in the off season. How could he get to the bank every day?"

"Your reporter buddy stops by for a few minutes some days. Joe goes then."

"I didn't know that." I of course knew George worked at least a few hours every week at Java Jolt, but couldn't imagine he'd go out of his way for Joe. Anyone who knows both of the auburn-haired men has been expecting a blow-up. They've never gotten along.

"You want help?" Lester asked.

"With what?"

"Don't gimme that. Investigating. We're a good team. Remember the booze operation?"

I shook my head. "I'm not investigating anything."

Lester stabbed the folded newspaper with his forefinger. "Accordin' to Tiffany, you almost got run down yesterday. Had to be because of what you saw."

I would have groaned, but my mouth was half-full of hamburger. I swallowed. "Reporters embellish."

Lester ignored this. "Old Bones Morehouse ain't gonna look too hard. He wants whoever shot at you to be long gone outta town."

"First, no one shot *at me*. Second, Morehouse is probably ten years younger than you are."

Lester, who is in his early fifties, waved aside my comment. "Don't matter. Where was Joe before here, do you think? When anybody asked he said he came here from the Midwest. I learned how to do Internet searches. His name is spelled funny. I don't find a Joe Regan anywhere but here."

I took my last bite of burger and spoke out of one side of my mouth. "Because he is here, not someplace else."

"You know what I mean. There's usually stuff pops up from when someone lived someplace else. At least when it's only a few years ago. Joe's only been here about four years."

I stared at Lester for a second. "I didn't know that."

"You wouldn't, 'cause you've only been back here what, three years? And you weren't here long when you lived here before."

I certainly had not known Joe when I spent my junior year of high school with Aunt Madge in Ocean Alley. Until Joe told Sergeant Morehouse he used to live in Kansas, I had not given any thought to how long Joe had been in town. If I had, I would have assumed he'd been here longer than four years. He seemed to know everyone. But he would, since Java Jolt would have brought him into contact with more people than if he'd worked as an accountant or something.

"I wonder why he opened a coffee shop," I mused. "He isn't overly friendly."

"See, you're startin'." Lester leaned part way across the table. "We find out what he did before and we maybe know why someone wanted to off him."

I changed the subject. "How's Ramona? Last email she sent said her graphic design course was even more work than she thought it would be." *I really miss her.*

"I like what she draws, especially when it's a caricature of the president of the Board of Realtors. I don't know why she's gotta start using computers for art stuff." He brightened. "Maybe Max could talk to her and she could kinda draw a suspect."

I slurped once more on my straw and stood. "Not going to get involved in this one, Lester."

"Gimme a break. If it wasn't for Max your ass would be grass and that SUV woulda been the lawnmower."

Ass would be grass? "I have to go to the office to pick up paperwork for an appraisal."

"I'm gonna do an open house at Fielding's this Sunday. Stop by if you wanna plan anything."

"Don't think so, Lester."

I gave him a ta-ta wave and headed for the courthouse. Papers would be on file for when Joe opened Java Jolt. Maybe there would be a clue about his financing or what he did before Java Jolt.

I COULD HAVE walked to the courthouse, but Lester would have noticed where I was going and followed. *What a busybody.*

I parked in the lot to one side of the building. Miller County has less land than any county in New Jersey, and its courthouse is also the smallest in the state. As I walked up the stone steps toward the first-floor offices I frequent, I glanced at the groomed lawn. Though not large, there are always flowers that befit the season. It looked as if someone had just planted a bunch of greenhouse-raised mums.

Usually I go to the Registrar of Deeds, which has information on all the properties in town and what they sold for. Staff in that office could tell me where to learn more about Java Jolt, but they all know me. They'd want to know what I was doing.

I meandered toward the Office of the Clerk of Court, stopping only to talk to a friend of Aunt Madge's, whose name I could not remember, to assure her I was fine.

The woman bobbed her head so hard I thought the bun on top would shake off. "What strange mishaps you get into young lady. If that Iraqi vet man hadn't been there, you could have been deader than a fish left on the beach after high tide."

I told her I was very fortunate. When it looked as if she wanted to talk more I fibbed. "I need to pick up some documents for an appraisal today. Thanks for the kind words."

To my back, she added, "Come visit us at First Prez this Sunday."

I turned to flash her a smile and walked to the counter in the clerk's office. The young assistant smiled at me. "Is Mrs. Finley trying to save your soul?"

A man's voice said, "She's beyond hope."

I turned to see George. *Nuts!* George would realize I wasn't doing appraisal work.

"You shouldn't talk to yourself," I told him, and turned back to the blonde assistant. She was about twenty-five, with very alert green eyes. "Where would I find information filed on a local business?"

George sidled next to me, and I could almost feel him smirking.

"That's funny, George just asked me the same question." She looked at him and back to me.

I smiled at her. "The insurance office probably wants to see how fast George can get a question answered."

"Oh, umm." Her nametag said Jessica, and she now looked confused.

"She's kidding," George said. "They already know I'm good."

I let my eyes travel heaven-ward and come back to look at Jessica. "I wanted to know if Joe Regan was the first owner of Java Jolt."

Jessica raised one eyebrow. "Everyone wants to know about Joe and Java Jolt. Do you know if he's okay?"

"Yeah," George chimed in. "Any word?"

I looked at George, who looked at Jessica and grinned. I said. "I heard he had surgery yesterday and it went well."

Jessica looked relieved. "Oh, that's good. He's where we all go for morning coffee."

I was tempted to tell Jessica that coffee was not the most important thing, but since I go to Java Jolt regularly, I didn't.

"Do you suppose someone will run it for him while he's sick?" Jessica asked.

I looked at George, who said. "That'd be a good idea."

He and I both looked at Jessica and she gave us a blank

stare for a couple of seconds. "Oh, business records. A long time ago people filed business registration papers at the courthouse, but it's all done online now. I can give you the web site."

I tried to hide my disappointment. "Okay, thanks." I took a small notepad from the side pocket of my purse, and George pulled one from his shirt pocket. I noticed he still carried a thin reporter's notebook, which has the spiral on top.

Jessica rattled off a New Jersey government web site and added, "I think if they're small, like Joe, they mostly file stuff for taxes. But you can still see a list of businesses on the web."

We thanked her and walked back to the courthouse entry foyer, which has a few benches and doors that lead to other offices.

George was in reporter-grilling-source mode. "What have you been up to? Scoobie said you were going to leave this alone."

I stifled a sigh as I sat on a bench. George plopped next to me. "Are you going to tell Scoobie what I'm doing?"

"He might know you're up to something," George said, eyes laughing at me. "He called on his break this morning and made me swear to tell him if you wanted me to help you."

"And you, uh, already promised?"

George gave a half laugh, half whoop. "He is my best friend. Plus, I actually thought you might lay off, since you're only walking around today because of Max."

I stretched my arm out and back. "My elbow's still stiff, but I'm fine." When George didn't say anything, I added, "Okay, I promise I'll tell Scoobie what I did today when I see him tonight. If you'll tell me what you found out."

"Fair enough, if you'll really *do* it."

"I said I would." My tone was testy, and when George just looked at me I continued in a low tone. "I went to Neptune this morning. To see Joe."

"Even I wouldn't have the balls to do that."

"Only because you know people would recognize you as someone who used to be with the *Ocean Alley Press*."

"True. What did you find out?"

I described how Joe looked and that it was hard for him to talk.

"Go figure," George said.

"You want to hear this?" I took his silence as consent and continued.

When I finished telling him about Morehouse and Dana, he spoke slowly. "So, Joe was in Kansas, and some Kansas robber's fingerprint was on the door to Java Jolt."

"Yep. I didn't know he'd only been here for four years. Does he ever talk about where he was before that?"

"Not really, but some of his expressions are kind of...farmish."

"Farmish?"

"Like when they talked about building more dunes to protect the town, he said the mayor and council members were shutting the barn door after the horse got out."

"New Jersey has farms, too," I mused. "He never mentioned Kansas?"

"Nope. I've heard a couple of people ask if he grew up around here, and all he says was he bummed around the Midwest before he came here. He and I don't do a lot of chit-chat."

"Mmm. You have a key to Java Jolt?"

"Yeah, but police tape is still up." George eyed me for a moment. "I suppose I could tell Morehouse I want to get the place cleaned up for when Joe comes back."

"That's a good idea."

"Actually, I should. There's probably food that'll need to be eaten or tossed out before it rots." George stood. "You check the computer stuff. I'll swing by the station to ask if I can go in." He pointed a finger at me. "And tell Scoobie."

George walked away. I wanted to ask for leftover food that wasn't spoiled, but the health department says food we give away has to be fresh or in its original packaging. A glance at my phone said there was time to stop by Harvest for All to check on our supply of key items that kids eat. Tomorrow would be a donation day, and there are some things I'm not willing to be low on, even if I have to personally buy green beans or kids' cereal now and then.

CHAPTER SEVEN

GIVEN THE EVENTS OF THE last couple of days, I peered in the Harvest for All storefront window before I unlocked the door. I could have gone into the church and walked through it to the community room area to enter the food pantry, but that would mean talking to Reverend Jamison's secretary. She usually has a snide comment about some aspect of my behavior.

The pantry looks like a dry cleaner's shop except with shelves of food behind the counter instead o f racks of clothes. There are a couple of huge refrigerators in the back. They were a bequest from a good friend of Lance's, and enable us to accept donations of milk, eggs, fruit and, during the holidays, frozen turkeys and ham.

Though it can be a hectic place, when it's empty the pantry is as quiet as the church. I picked up a clipboard and pencil from the counter and started a quick inventory.

The aisle with pasta, cereal, and dried beans would not have to be restocked before our next delivery of supplies from the food bank in Lakewood. The canned food aisle was another matter. I'd probably have to ask Mr. Markle to sell us some applesauce and canned corn or peas at cost.

A knock on the door made me look up. We have to have a pretty strict policy about only providing food on the three days a week that we distribute, but if someone's desperate we'll give them a couple of canned items. If we're in the pantry.

Two people stood there. One was a regular customer, a women in her late fifties who had no local family. She gave me a sort of sheepish look. The other woman was much younger and maybe five-four. She looked over her shoulder as if nervous.

It's too bad some people are ashamed to come.

I unlocked the door and looked at the unfamiliar woman. "Hi. I'm Jolie."

The new woman seemed surprised by my friendliness. "Oh. I'm, uh, Connie. Are you allowed to give me anything today?"

The woman I knew, Mary Margaret, said, "I saw her getting soup at the market, and she didn't have enough money. I told her it was okay to come here."

I opened the door to let them come in. "Good for you Mary Margaret. Are you okay until tomorrow?"

She nodded, and turned to leave. "I'll be here bright and early." She looked at the younger woman. "See, it's okay."

I shut the door and smiled at Connie as I walked behind the counter. "Tomorrow's a day we pass out, so I can only give you a few items today. Are you registered with Salvation Army or maybe Family Services? We can give you food only a couple of times if you don't register with anyone."

Connie stood on the customer side of the counter and looked at the rows of shelves. "Wow. You have a lot."

"We feed a lot of families. Would you like a bag of rice and cans of vegetables and fruit?"

She appeared to be more comfortable, and her smile was engaging. "Yes, please. I left my Medicaid card at home, but I can bring it tomorrow."

"Perfect." I walked behind the counter and made for the fruit. "Applesauce or peaches?"

"Peaches." She was the epitome of politeness. "Is this your full-time job?"

"No. We're all volunteers. Peas, beans, or corn?"

"Um, corn. Do you have to be here every day?"

"No, in fact I usually only help with distribution one day a week. I chair our committee that raises funds and things, so that keeps me kind of busy."

"What's your real job?"

I had finished loading my arms with the cans and bag of rice and set them on the counter. "I'm a real estate appraiser. We help figure out what a house is worth when it's being sold."

She nodded, then looked more interested. "Were you in the paper today?"

My smile was grim. "Yep. The paper made it sound as if someone was trying to run into me, but there's no way to be sure of that."

Connie frowned. "No one should run over a nice lady like you."

I smiled as I put her items in a plastic bag. "You tell 'em, kid." *Kid, she's probably thirty or thirty-five.* She had a kind of waifish look and her blue jeans were too loose. That's often a sign of what policy makers call food insecurity and we at Harvest for All call hunger.

That earned me another smile as she accepted the bag. "Thanks a lot."

"Sure. Tomorrow is a day we're open in the morning. You can see the hours on the door, or I'll write them down for you. You can come once or twice a month. If you come once we provide more, but then we then really have to stick to once a month."

"Sure, I get it." She turned to leave.

"Connie." She turned to face me. "You have a place to sleep? If not a couple of the churches..."

"I'm good." She walked toward the door without looking back. She left, and was soon out of sight.

Usually someone says what brought them to Harvest for All. Not that they have to. But they often want to emphasize their lack of money was beyond their control. Connie's clothes were well-worn, but not dirty, and her dark blonde hair was clean. I pegged her as someone who was having a short-term problem, and was glad that when I left my husband I had Aunt Madge and her well stocked kitchen to go to.

AT THE APPRAISAL office I picked up information on two appraisal requests. One was actually from a local bank. So many banks have consolidated that more than half of our requests for work come from bigger banks around New Jersey, or even other states.

It sounded as if a car pulled up in front of the house. *Don't be so nervous*. I decided I wasn't nervous, just careful. The driver of the dark blue sedan was not a large person, but I couldn't tell if it was a man or a woman. The person consulted a piece of paper, looked at Harry's house, and then pulled back into traffic. *It's nothing. Someone trying to find an address.*

I glanced at my watch. It was almost two-forty-five. Scoobie would get off work soon. I love that we live together now. Sometimes it feels as if we always did. The only disadvantage is that he more or less expects to know where I am when he gets off work. I know it's just him being companionable, but I've gotten used to being pretty independent. I wish he had what I think of as a more traditional work schedule.

After making a photocopy of the two emailed appraisal requests and checking the fax for anything from Lester, I left for home. I had just pulled into the graveled section of my small lawn that passes for a driveway when Scoobie drove up and parked next to my Toyota.

He got out of his recently purchased used VW and waved a plastic bag at me. "I brought dinner."

Since it was from the vet, I knew it was Skunkie Delight, the smelly food that Pebbles eats. "You want it warmed up?"

He laughed. "Pebbles might."

Scoobie can't talk about individual patients in any way that would identify them, but he usually has a story or two from his day. Today's was about a four-year old who didn't want his head x-rayed.

"He was sure the x-ray machine would suck his brain out. Where do you think he got that idea?"

"TV space show, probably." I unlocked the front door. "What did you tell him?"

"That I'd put an invisible cover over the part he said was the machine's mouth, and it would prevent any sucking."

"His parents will love that."

Scoobie shrugged. "They should keep a better eye on him. He was balancing on the back of the sofa, pretending it was a tight rope."

"Tough job, parenting," I said. I was trying to decide if I should tell him about my day before or after he had his usual snack of a banana with peanut butter. After, I decided.

While he changed, I mashed a banana in a bowl. He puts on the amount of peanut butter he wants and sticks it in the microwave for fifteen or twenty seconds. I think it's gross.

Scoobie came into the kitchen and picked up the bowl from the counter. "Thanks. I'll handle the haute cuisine part."

He heated his concoction and looked at me as he stirred the results. "You look pensive. Have a tough appraisal?"

"Nope. Thought I'd tell you about my day while you eat." He stopped eating midway through his bowl of banana and stared at me as I recounted the trip to the hospital.

"So, Joe was really pale, but he looked better than I expected," I finished. I had decided to let him think I was in the room when Morehouse saw Joe, and that's how I heard about the fingerprints the police found in Java Jolt.

Scoobie took a bite and swallowed. "You know what this means?"

"That Joe might have, maybe, been involved in..."

"No." Scoobie's retort was quick. "That *we'd* be nuts to try to talk to Joe about any of this. Unless *we* want our petard run over by the next SUV that aims at us."

"Is that the editorial we?" I asked, trying to be funny.

"Come on, Jolie, is it really worth risking all of this," he gestured around the living room with his spoon, "to figure out why Joe got shot?"

I stared at him. For a second I thought he meant he'd leave, and I felt a quick chill. I decided he just meant we had a nice house, a nice life. "I don't want to risk anything. I just went to visit him."

Scoobie gave me a kind of evil-eye look, but before he said anything else we heard footsteps on the bungalow's porch.

Unfortunately, I recognized the sharp rap on the door.

"Morehouse," I said to Scoobie, as I stood.

"What did you do now?"

I made a face. "Very funny." I opened the door. "Hello Sergeant, what a lovely surprise."

Morehouse snorted as he walked in. "Yeah, like you think so. Hey Scoobie, glad you're here."

That doesn't sound good.

Scoobie held out his mostly empty bowl so Morehouse could see the contents. "Want any?"

Morehouse accepted my gesture and sat in the rocking chair, which faced the couch Scoobie and I now sat on together. Morehouse eyed the bowl again. "That's grosser than some of the stuff on the sidewalk outside the Sandpiper on Saturday night."

Scoobie laughed and my stomach did a roil. "Nice."

"Sorry. Just wanted to give you some advice, Jolie."

"Orders work better," Scoobie said.

"Not in my experience with her," Morehouse said.

"I'm in the room." I looked at both of them and then back at Morehouse. "What's up?"

"I wanna be sure you don't nose around about Joe. Fingerprints at Java Jolt, which you can't tell anybody about, show that a pretty unsavory character was at his back door, probably the day he got shot."

Scoobie looked at me, and I avoided his gaze. I knew he was thinking that Morehouse had already told me this in person.

"Anyone I know?" I asked.

"Not unless you're pals with the FBI in another state."

Rats. He isn't going to tell me anything I don't know.

Morehouse tapped his foot for a second. "I know neither one of you tells the other what to do, but I think it's good you both hear this."

I didn't want the conversation to linger on the person who was in the store. "You'd better tell George. I saw him at the courthouse today and he was thinking of talking to you about going in there to clean up the place."

Morehouse looked surprised. "Him and Joe don't like each other."

"He's worked there part-time since he got fired from the *Ocean Alley Press*," I said.

"In addition to doing stuff for the insurance agency," Scoobie said.

"Why didn't I know that?" Morehouse asked.

"Because you don't spend three dollars for a cup of coffee," Scoobie said.

"That's for sure." Morehouse looked at me. "I'll talk to George. You get my drift?"

"Yep. Thanks."

"Butt out," Morehouse said.

"I'll remind her," Scoobie threw in.

I stood. "If you see Joe, tell him we said hi."

Morehouse looked at Scoobie. "I'm gettin' kicked out."

Scoobie grinned. "It happens."

After perfunctory good-byes, we walked back to the living room and Scoobie looked at me. "Why do I think I didn't get the full story about what you did today?"

Jazz wrapped herself around my ankle and Pebbles, who had gone under our bed when Morehouse knocked, stuck her head around the corner from the hallway.

"I think I forgot to mention I wasn't exactly sitting by Joe's bed when Morehouse talked to him."

"Where were you? Listening at the door?"

"In the closet in Joe's room."

It was very quiet in our house for the rest of the evening.

CHAPTER EIGHT

THE NEXT MORNING I went to the library to search for business records. I also wanted to search the *Ocean Alley Press* index for material that related to Java Jolt. Usually the paper has articles on new businesses. Maybe in an interview Joe mentioned something I didn't already know.

Normally I would search on my laptop. However, Scoobie and I don't usually keep secrets, and if I'm not on my laptop, he would feel free to use it. I don't use his because he bought it used and it's slower than waiting for a Harvest Moon to rise. Scoobie certainly would not snoop around my files, but when you type in a web address sometimes a list of recent sites visited pops up.

I didn't want him to know the websites I'd prowled, and I only knew how to erase all site history rather than individual ones. Finding no history would look weird if he used the Internet on my computer. I didn't want to have to lie if he asked me questions about the erased history. *Bad enough that I'm creating the history.*

It was with a mild pang of guilt that I waved hello to Daphne, a librarian who was in my year in high school and volunteers for Harvest for All. *I'm not doing anything I said I wouldn't. I'm just looking at information.*

The other side of my brain had a comment. *You're kidding yourself. If you don't plan to discuss what you're looking for with Scoobie, you're lying by omission.*

I hate it when both sides of an issue float across my brain

when I'm trying to focus.

First was a review of the paper's index starting four years ago and moving toward the present. Three years and eight months ago, an article that featured the Ocean Alley Chamber of Commerce president of that time said the town "was ecstatic to have an independent coffee shop open in time for the upcoming summer season."

While there were several handsome photos of the Java Jolt interior, which had once been an arcade Scoobie and I snuck to sometimes during junior year, I found little personal information about Joe. It said that he had considered joining his "family's Midwest agricultural business" but decided that he wanted a chance to be near the ocean for a while.

Why don't they even name the state he was from? A glance at the byline answered that question. Katherine Hargrove used to write what papers today call lifestyle articles for the *Ocean Alley Press*. She was the daughter of the paper's founder. Several times I'd heard George refer to her at Katty Kathy. He thought she was little more than a gossip columnist. And she was dead, so there would be no chance to see if Joe had provided more information than she had included in the article.

At least I knew the date Java Jolt opened. I moved from the microfilm machine that let me read older editions of the *Ocean Alley Press* to a nearby computer. I began an online search of New Jersey business records. I quickly ascertained that since Joe was not a large business, there were few requirements that he give the state information.

The business records site required me to pay for anything I wanted, other than the list of businesses that popped up during my search. I didn't want to put in my credit card information, but couldn't think of an alternative.

That done, I had the paperwork Joe filed when he opened the business. It wasn't much. Just the date, address, type of business, and the fact that the expected number of employees was less than five. If he bought the building a realtor might know more. More likely he rented. Buying a building on the boardwalk, even a small one, would have cost a small fortune. Literally.

I was about to close the web page when a name jumped out at me. The owner was listed as James Rosen. *Excuse me?* Same initials, obviously, but definitely not Joe Regan.

Something in the back of my brain tried to move to the front, but was blocked. Probably by my somewhat guilty conscience. No amount of staring at the computer screen would bring the thought to mind.

Behind me a voice hissed. "Jolie, Jolie. I'm whispering."

I turned, and smiled. "Hi, Max. You look chipper."

He stared at me for a second, and then said simply, "I'm fine. Can I sit with you, Jolie? Sit with you?"

When I nodded, he moved the chair from the computer next to mine to be close to me.

That's it! "Max, when we were talking to Sergeant Morehouse, did you say something about Joe's name being different?"

"Dana. I told Dana."

"Right. I don't remember exactly what you said."

Max thought for a few seconds. "The man who was mad at Joe said Joe's name was different." He paused, and added, "Joe used a name that made him hard to find. Hard to find."

"Did the man say if Joe Regan was Joe's real name?"

"No. Do you want to go get a donut?"

"A...? Sure. You want to go to Newhart's Diner?" I asked.

He nodded. "It's for my sugar fix." As he sometimes does when he is repeating what someone has said to him, Max's words had a sort of sing-song cadence.

I exited the web browser, turned off the computer screen and stood. "Who told you you need a sugar fix?"

Max was examining the huge dictionary that sits on a podium. "Joe says that's why he gives me muffins." He lifted a batch of pages so the dictionary was open to a large color map and looked at me over his shoulder. "This is where Iraq is," he pointed to the Middle East, "and this is where we are."

"I'm glad you're here in New Jersey with me."

"Me too," he said, emphatically.

THOUGH WE SAT NEAR the rear of the diner, several people came over to talk to Max and me. Arnie gave Max his donut on the house -- a cake donut with chocolate icing and sprinkles. Arnie said it was because Max saved me.

"So Arnie," I asked, "how did you know it was Max?"

He shrugged. "Everybody knows. Same as always."

I did know how fast news traveled in Ocean Alley. I'd been pleased not to see Max's name in the paper, and was sorry if the driver of the SUV could learn who Max was.

I had just asked Max if he had heard from his friend Josh lately when an intense-sounding voice came from behind me. "Jolie Gentil. Why is it always you?"

Elmira Washington stood next to our booth. She goes to First Prez with Aunt Madge. With her short-cropped hair and straight spine, she brings to mind a drill sergeant. They, however, are more likeable. Now I knew who was spreading Max's name around.

"Hello, Elmira," I said. I looked across the table at Max. "You want one to take out, so you can eat it later?"

"Well?" Elmira's tone was even more demanding."

"Well what?"

"I asked you a question!" Her face had red splotches where there had been none a moment ago.

"No you didn't. You made a rude comment and tried to disguise it as a question." I looked at her directly, but did not smile.

"Well, I never!"

"Never what?" Max asked.

Elmira turned and marched to the door, hands at her sides and fists clenched.

I heard a chuckle behind me, and Arnie came into view. He's in his sixties, not too tall, and very trim Probably because he runs around the diner all day. "Pretty good, Jolie."

"Never what?" Max asked, again.

"It's an expression," Arnie said. "It means she doesn't like what Jolie said to her."

"She's trying to say nobody's ever talked to her as I just did," I added.

Max leaned across the table and whispered. "No one likes her."

WHEN I DROPPED Max at his house I offered to come in to be sure no one was there who had not been invited.

"No one bad will be there. I have locks on my windows."

His steps were confident as he walked into the house. I pulled away from the curb. There was no reason that the person who shot Joe should think Max had seen him at Java Jolt two days ago -- assuming it was the same person who tried to flatten me. I was the one who saw Joe just after he was shot, not Max. Still, I worried.

DR. WELBY HAD managed to get the Harvest for All Committee together for a brief evening meeting in the small conference room at the church. I almost wondered if he had contacted the others before he called me. Not that it mattered.

First Presbyterian is a traditional Protestant church made of brick, with white trim and steeple. Aunt Madge said they've been offered what she called substantial sums to sell the land and rebuild the church on the edge of town. I figure that's as likely as snow in August.

Behind the church, and a bit lower than the sacristy, is an attached flat-roofed building that houses Sunday School classrooms, a large community room, and the food pantry. One door of the pantry opens to the street and another to the hallway by the community room.

I talked to my good friend Lance Wilson as we waited for others to arrive. Lance is in his mid-nineties, with a mind much younger. His spirits are a lot better than a year ago. Then he'd been in a temporary apartment as his small home was renovated after water damage from Hurricane Sandy.

"Listen, Jolie, I think Sylvia and Monica are anxious that whatever we do this fall is a bit more...calm than the last couple of fundraisers."

I acknowledged his point with a nod. "I think the corn hole...I mean corn toss contest was a little rambunctious for them."

"To say nothing of the liquid string contest," Lance said, dryly.

Sylvia walked into the room. "We never need to talk about that again as far as I'm concerned."

Sylvia is efficient and has good ideas. Her posture is not the only thing rigid about her. She is the only person I've seen Scoobie be snotty with.

"Yes," I said, quickly. "We already agreed it would be more like a traditional canned food drive, with something fun combined with it. I think Dr. Welby has some ideas to try on us."

She gave a smug smile, and then her expression softened. "Have you heard anything about Joe?"

"Aunt Madge heard he's recovering okay." I was not about to imply that I'd seen him.

"Good to hear," Lance said, and Sylvia nodded.

Laughter at the far end of the hall announced Aretha and Monica. Aretha makes sure we reach into the poorest communities, and Monica sort of organizes the bake sales. They greeted us, and I noted Monica's cardigan was not buttoned up to her neck. I think of this as her relaxed look.

An exterior door banged and Dr. Welby's booming voice came to us. "I know Jolie will be on board with this."

I figured he had to be talking to Megan, who organizes most of our volunteers at the pantry itself. She is quiet, efficient, and steady as a rock.

"Evening Jolie," Dr. Welby said, as he entered the room.

For some reason, I decided to make a point of asserting that I was the chair. I'm not usually like that. I smiled at him as he sat at the other head of the small conference table, opposite me. "Aha. The spiritual guide is here. I wouldn't think of starting a meeting without you."

He gave me a broad smile.

"Where's Scoobie?" Lance asked.

"He had a meeting. He'll be late," Dr. Welby said. "And Daphne had to work at the library."

Scoobie grew up in Ocean Alley, and half the town knows that he more or less raised himself and then majored in marijuana when he went to college just after high school. Most of those people also know how hard Scoobie worked to get his life on track. He and George have used varying levels of encouragement to get me to go to Twelve Step meetings in the past. They think I have control issues or something ridiculous like that.

"So, thank you all for coming on short notice," I said.

Sylvia had a self-satisfied look.

"I know we're a bit behind in planning something for the fall," I began.

"I thought I might save you some time," Dr. Welby said. "We talked about a location for a kids' Halloween party. I have a surprise."

"I love surprises," I said, not sure I did.

He smiled at each of us, individually. You'd have thought he was a tech mogul introducing a new product. "I talked to my club. They would be happy to host us one week from Saturday."

"You mean the country club, on the edge of town?" Aretha asked.

When Dr. Welby and Sylvia nodded, Aretha said, slowly, "As I recall, we try to make these events some that our clientele will be comfortable attending. I'm not sure everyone plays golf there."

Dr. Welby literally waved aside her comment. "All the better. It will give some people exposure to things they don't usually see."

All Megan did was straighten in her chair, but everyone noticed. As a single mom with a teenage daughter, she was likely the kind of person Dr. Welby was referring to. "Perhaps not everyone will be able to dress for your occasion."

People don't actually turn green, but Dr. Welby sort of did. "I don't mean to be condescending. I mean, we'll be in costumes. I thought it would be a way to get some wealthier donors. Some of my friends said they would be willing to help..."

Megan relaxed her shoulders and threw him a lifeline. "That could bring in extra money for the holidays. Will you arrange for transportation for those who live closer to downtown? The bus doesn't go to the country club."

CHAPTER NINE

BY THE END OF last evening's Harvest for All meeting we had agreed to publicize a costume donation day for the food pantry, with the day after it being for people who needed a costume to select one. I was concerned that we might run out of costumes on the giveaway day, but Megan said there were probably two hundred costumes for sale in the Salvation Army Thrift Store. We could dash over there and buy a bunch if we had to.

My afternoon courthouse search for comparable sales for a two-story colonial took my mind off the party and deterred worry about Max. Plus, there was time to think about when I could talk to Joe again. After four days in the hospital, I thought he'd be able to handle a visitor. Whether he wanted to talk to me was another issue.

As I walked down the courthouse steps a good-looking man in perhaps his mid-thirties came up to me. "Ms. Genteel?" he asked.

When someone butchers my name, I know it's a stranger. "It's a French pronunciation, long E sound at the end. Zho-lee Zhan-tee," I said. "I don't think we've met."

"Talbot Peters," he said, extending a hand.

From his dark-blonde hair and height of about five-ten or so I expected a firm clasp, but was rewarded with a limp handshake that was quickly pulled back.

"I'm an acquaintance of Joe's. I read about the shooting

and drove over from Trenton, but he wasn't in the hospital here."

I motioned to a nearby bench and we walked toward it. "Yes, he was transferred to a larger facility in a near-by town." I didn't know the guy, so wasn't about to say where.

He smiled as we sat, a seemingly practiced smile that went to eyes that were such dark blue they were almost violet. An odd color for a man, I thought.

"I'm not the bad guy. I supply some of Joe's paper goods." When he could tell I was still unsure what to tell him, Peters added, "Shooters stay away from the courthouse."

I relaxed. "Good to know. I don't know a lot about his condition, but he did come through surgery well and the police say he'll recover."

"That's great. Listen, fall is a slow season for me. Everybody gets stocked up in the spring, but the seasonal businesses are closing. Do you know if he needs any help at the coffee shop?"

"I'm not sure, but I think I know a way to find out." I explained that George had checked with the police to be sure it was okay to go into Java Jolt.

"How do I get hold of this George guy?" he asked.

I gave him George's mobile number. It wasn't until Talbot Peters' car was pulling out of the courthouse parking lot that I wondered how he knew my name.

GEORGE, SCOOBIE, AND I were on the couch in the bungalow's living room at seven PM. It's times like this when I especially miss Ramona. Life is always better with a girlfriend in the room, and the four of us usually have dinner together at least once a week. *Four weeks isn't that long, and it's already been more than two.*

"So, George said, "we can open Java Jolt if Joe gives permission, which he will. He's not independently wealthy."

"But who would run it?" Scoobie asked. "You're only part-time there."

"Jolie's been recruiting." He explained the call from Talbot Peters. "I threw away a boatload of stale pastries today. I also found his list of suppliers and called them to say I'd be placing orders for a while.

"What about your work at the insurance company?" I asked.

George had a look I would characterize as shifty.

"What are *you* up to?" Scoobie asked, looking at George.

"Okay, you know that to become a private detective in New Jersey I have to work for two years in an investigative capacity."

"And," I threw in, "you're annoyed that they won't count your years pestering people for the *Ocean Alley Press*."

"Yeah, but I kind of have a deal with All Things Insurance. I have to put in my two years, and of course do some work for them. Like making sure something reported as stolen really is."

"How can you do that?" Scoobie asked.

"I can't, one hundred percent. But a few weeks ago I found a ten thousand dollar diamond necklace that was pawned in Hoboken and not stolen from Ocean Grove."

"Wow," I said.

"Don't repeat that," he said, quickly. "It's company business."

"So what does that have to do with running Java Jolt?" Scoobie asked.

"My deal with the guys at the insurance company is that I can have a flexible schedule. And maybe not always put in forty hours a week, since they know I have good investigative skills. It's an hourly wage, not a salary."

I stared at him. "Do you get a bonus for saving them ten-thousand dollars?"

"It's my job," George said, with a shrug. Then his eyes grew brighter. "And since I can't be at Java Jolt full-time, that's where you guys come in."

"Oh, no," Scoobie said.

"C'mon, Scoob, just a couple nights a week."

"Will Joe be there at all?" I asked.

Scoobie gave me a look that telegraphed exasperation.

"You know," George said, "if he showed up with his sling it might be good for business."

"Oh yeah," Scoobie said. "Maybe draw people with guns to entertain the customers."

I laughed, and so did George.

"It seems like the last place the shooter would go," I said, looking at Scoobie. Then I looked at George. "I can help some in the mornings, but not every day. Most people want an appraisal in the afternoons, for some reason." I've always thought this was so they could get their house picked up.

"Okay," George sat up straighter. "And Lester said..."

"I'm not working with Lester!"

"Are you kidding? That's how I got him to agree." George's expression was a cross between disappointed and pleading.

"You've been busy," Scoobie said, quietly. "Especially for someone who doesn't like Joe a helluva lot."

George took a breath that was almost a sigh. "I don't. He's

abrupt, even when you work there. No chit chat."

"Maybe he was hiding something," I said, dryly.

"Yeah, well, he offered me part-time work when I really needed a boost. I feel like I owe him."

"And maybe," Scoobie said, "you wanted to use your investigative skills to see if anything is hidden in Java Jolt."

George gave a quick grin. "I made a good start on that today."

None of us said anything for a few seconds, and then Scoobie spoke. "Okay, I get it. But I don't want Jolie working alone."

Normally I would take offense if someone implied I couldn't do something or make my own choices, but I knew Scoobie was thinking safety, not control. "Lester," I sighed. "Make sure he leaves his cigar in his office. It stinks even when it's not lit."

GEORGE HAD NOMINATED me to visit Joe the next day to get permission to open Java Jolt. Scoobie wasn't keen on it but I didn't need any encouragement. Joe could answer some questions, and if anyone from law enforcement came by, I had a legitimate reason to be in Joe's room.

It was drizzling lightly as I drove to Neptune, so I stayed in the right lane, much to the annoyance of some other drivers in the lane who seemed to want to go ten miles above the limit. One of the few lessons I remember from driver's ed is that highways are most dangerous when just getting damp, because any oil on the road is more slippery before the pavement is thoroughly wet. Eventually there were several cars behind me, all willing to go the speed limit.

On my mind as I walked into the hospital was how to find

Joe. When I was in the closet a few days ago, the nurse called Joe Mr. Smith. *Really original.* I figured that if Joe wasn't supposed to be known by his own name, even Mr. Smith wasn't likely to be on the hospital's list of patients. Instead of asking, I went back to the Step-Down Unit and walked toward the nurses' station. When I got close to it I looked in the room that was Joe's a few days ago. Empty.

A man's voice greeted me. "Can I help you, Miss?"

The nametag said, "Ronald N., RN."

"Do people tease you about being Ronald N., RN?" I asked.

His look of suspicion turned to tolerance. "Not if they know me."

"Sorry, guess it gets old." I nodded to the patient room. "My friend Joe was in there a couple of days ago. But he wasn't under his name, he was called Mr. Smith."

Ronald-the-RN adopted a very professional demeanor. "We don't give out information without a patient's permission."

"I'm offering, not asking. Some of his friends want to run his coffee shop for him while he's recovering. We should really have his permission, though."

"Hmm." Ronald pointed to the waiting area a short distance away. "Have a seat."

I walked down the hall and sat, noting the magazines were the same dog-eared ones I'd seen the last time I was here. *No wonder germs get spread.*

I had barely sat when Ronald-the-RN came back, holding a portable phone to his ear. He looked at me. "Yep, looks like her. Uh-huh." He ended the call. "Sergeant Morehouse says to call him. He was pretty adamant about *now*."

I rolled my eyes and thanked him. Ronald left.

I opened the phone conversation with Morehouse with, "I have you on speed-dial."

"My lucky day. What are you doin' there?"

I explained George's plan to open Java Jolt, and that I had the more flexible schedule this morning, so I came to talk to Joe.

"How'd you even know Joe was well enough to talk?"

Uh oh. I improvised. "Aunt Madge."

"Cripes." Morehouse paused, then sighed. "He gets out in a day or so anyway, and it's not like he's under police protection." He gave me Joe's room number and said not to pry or pester him.

"I never pester."

Morehouse grunted and hung up with his trademark lack of good-bye.

Joe's room was on the same floor, but on the regular Med/Surg Unit. I walked toward the nurses' station there and spoke to a woman close to the counter. "Sergeant Morehouse gave me Mr. Smith's room number. I thought I'd tell you that before I went in."

She was about my age, in no-nonsense blue scrubs rather than the flowery ones some of the other nurses wore. "He's all yours."

I raised an eyebrow at her. "Sounds like he's being himself."

She shook her head and walked away.

His door was ajar, but the curtain was mostly closed, so I knocked. When no one responded, I said, "Joe? It's Jolie."

"Figures. You can come in," he said.

I walked to the partially open curtain and looked in at

him. Joe was in bed, but in a full sitting position, with the newspaper on the sheet in front of him. No lines ran in or out of him.

"You look a lot better than the last time I saw you."

"Chest tube is out. It sucked air out of my lung for a couple of days while it started to heal." He gave a fleeting smile. "At first I thought I dreamed you were here. Then I was pretty sure you told me Max stayed with you and Scoobie. I couldn't have imagined that."

I smiled in return and nodded at a chair a few feet from his bed. "Can I sit? I won't stay long."

"Yeah. Hey, are you okay? Father Teehan brought me a couple days of the *Ocean Alley Press*. I saw about your accident, or whatever it was."

"I was really lucky. If Max hadn't been…"

"Max! I should have known he was the person they didn't identify." Joe seemed to almost shrink into the bed.

"He's fine. His reflexes are terrific." I paused. "It seemed like they were aiming, but you never know. Could have been someone who was drunk or something. Try not to worry about it."

"I'm trying not to worry about a lot of things."

A lot of things?

Joe drew a slow breath in and out and attempted a smile. "This is the first day I've felt almost normal." He nodded his head at the arm in a sling. "Except for this."

I was tempted to say *and the bullet wound*, but I didn't. "I'm actually here as George's emissary."

"Oh, great."

"He got permission from Sergeant Morehouse to go into Java Jolt and clean out old muffins and stuff, so it didn't stink, and..."

"Gee, that's terrific."

It was the first time I'd seen Joe look genuinely pleased at something. "He said to tell you he was glad to do it. And he had an idea. Even if you can get back to work in a few days, it'll be awhile before you can lift those big coffee pots."

"No kidding."

I outlined George's plan to train several of us to work at Java Jolt. "It might be more limited hours than you usually have, but at least it would be open."

"That could work," he said slowly, "but the place doesn't bring in a lot of money for salaries. I can't let..."

"Volunteers. Besides," I grinned at him, "I bet I get better tips than you do."

"*That* wouldn't be hard." He eyed me, apparently thinking. "You know, there are times I could work alone, too. Once the morning rush is over, one huge pot of coffee and another of hot water last for a few hours."

I was tempted to say the coffee occasionally tasted like it, but didn't. "I just have one question. It's safe, right? No one's really looking for you?"

Joe was somber. "I didn't know the guy who tried to rob me. I shoved him hard and he ran off. Not likely he'll try again. Keep the back door locked, though."

I nodded. "Was he, uh, the one who shot you?"

Joe shook his head. "I don't know. The sun was behind the shooter, so it was in my eyes. All I have is an image of a guy. I don't even remember anyone shooting me."

"When I was here the day after you were shot, I also heard what Sergeant Morehouse and Dana talked to you about."

Joe frowned. "You eavesdropped?"

"Not on purpose. I mean, I didn't want Morehouse to know I was here, and there was no way to leave. So I kind of hid in the closet."

He looked half-amused, half-angry. "You probably remember more about that conversation than I do."

"He was mostly giving you information. About fingerprints on the Java Jolt back door."

Joe nodded. "He was here again yesterday. I didn't know the person he was talking about."

"Who was it?"

Joe thought for a moment. "Barney somebody, I think. Didn't mean anything to me."

"So," I asked, "not someone you knew before you moved to Ocean Alley?"

Now Joe was one hundred percent irritated. "People seem to forget I'm the victim here. For all I know, or Morehouse knows, those prints could belong to some druggie who was testing all the alley doors to see if one was unlocked."

"That's a good point," I mused. "Did you ask the police if they checked other doors?"

Joe's expression relaxed somewhat. "Why don't you ask them?"

"I'm not supposed to have heard that conversation, remember?"

He shrugged, then winced and adjusted his arm in the sling. "Maybe I will."

"I'm sorry to bug you," I began.

"Right," Joe muttered.

"It's just...odd that those two things, the person in the store and the shooting, would happen to you, isn't it?" *And that you seemed to have gone to Mr. Markle's store to hide between the time you shoved the guy and he shot you.*

"For once you agree with Morehouse. I figure the robber was super angry that I shoved him out the back door." Joe and I stared at each other for several seconds, and he looked away.

"It's a good thing the guy didn't follow you into Mr. Markle's store."

Joe looked almost startled. "How did...oh, I saw you there, right? I'm still kind of foggy about what all happened that day."

"For two seconds." I tried for mild levity. "I'm glad I didn't walk out with you."

"Damn." Joe seemed to be considering something, but then said nothing more.

"So, I'll tell George he can set the hours, shall I?"

"That'd be great. Tell him, tell him he's still an a-hole sometimes, but I really appreciate it."

I laughed. "Probably the kind of reaction he'd expect." I picked up my purse, which I had placed on the floor next to the chair, and stood. "I'll let you get some rest."

"Thanks for coming over...oh, tell George if he takes the money to the bank they'll let him deposit it. He can keep out cash for supplies or whatever."

"He and Scoobie are pretty innovative. And George will keep track."

"Not worried about that."

"So, when I tell George he's still an a-hole, I'll add that you trust him.

Joe smiled slightly. He leaned his head into the pillow and looked frustrated, or maybe depressed. "He'll get your drift."

I stood. "Get some rest." I had planned my exit question, so I turned back just as I got to the curtain. "Aunt Madge said to ask you what part of Kansas? One of her aunts lived in a little town called Seneca a very long time ago."

"How did you know...?"

"The closet, remember?"

He shook his head a bit. "Oh, and the paper. Kansas City most recently. Did a lot of odd jobs, you know, day labor. Then I decided the beach would be better."

"Better coffee for Ocean Alley, too." I left.

I THOUGHT AS I drove back to Ocean Alley. George wanted permission to open Java Jolt, but what I'd wanted was intelligence, so to speak. More than George wanted it, now that he's not a reporter. If I was going to volunteer at Java Jolt, for tips no less, I'd spend some time with Joe. Lots of hours to wheedle information, including who James Rosen was. I had intended to ask about the name during the visit, but it would have meant admitting I'd researched Joe's background. The few questions I'd asked had annoyed him enough, so I'd dropped the idea for now.

I put on my turn signal to pull into a parking spot by Steele Appraisals and a car's brakes screeched behind me. I looked in my rear view mirror, glad not to have been rear-ended. A man wearing a stocking cap gave me the finger, backed up quickly, and then roared past me.

And people say I'm impatient.

As I walked onto Harry's porch, something about Joe's appearance occurred to me. His roots were showing, just a little. *His hair isn't auburn, it's brown.*

CHAPTER TEN

WE WORKED OUR TAILS off for two days to get Java Jolt ready to reopen. Much was training time for Lester, Scoobie, and me. We were not always the best students.

Sometimes George's former boss feels bad about firing him. He as much as told him so a couple months after he did it. Not that he would change his mind. His remorse was probably why the *Ocean Alley Press* editor turned our announcement about reopening Java Jolt into a brief article on the front page.

We were swamped when the doors opened at seven AM. By nine-thirty it was finally getting calmer. Despite having had some training the day before, it was apparent neither Lester nor I knew how to operate even the milk steamer well.

Lance had stopped by and he began picking up used cups and napkins from the tables. "Maybe you could make a sign that says no fancy drinks from seven to nine. That's the only time you really had trouble."

I didn't think that would go over too well. "Maybe. Most days George'll be here when we open. He knows how to work all this stuff." I gestured at the array of machines that lined the wall behind the counter. *Who knew coffee could be so complicated?*

Lester's voice came from the supply closet. "I gotta talk to those insurance guys. If they'll let George be here when we open, I could give them one percent off my commission if I ever sell their house or the office."

Lester walked out of the closet carrying a large bag of sugar. He had come dressed in a collared shirt, and thankfully had a tee-shirt under it. My sense was he'd have removed the outer shirt when he got hot even if he hadn't been wearing a tee-shirt. *Thank heavens for large favors.*

Lester is famous for being cheap. Lance finished dropping the trash in the can, brushed his hands together briefly, and turned to look at Lester and me, eyes twinkling. "You probably don't want that discount business getting around."

"You ain't kiddin'." Lester shook a finger at me. "That's whaddyacallit, proprietary information."

"Like I'd do something so you'd send Harry and me less business." I picked up my now cold cup of tea and made a face as I sipped it.

"The tea Joe has here tastes like something you could pick up in the dog park," Lester said.

I cringed. Lance threw back his head and laughed. "On that note, I'm heading home. I'm an early gull, but I haven't bussed trays in years."

I walked to the customer side of the counter and kissed Lance on the cheek. "You're the best."

"Jolie, could you help...no, I can do it." Lester had opened the ten pound bag of sugar and aimed it one of the glass dispensers that customers use to add sugar to their drinks.

"Lester, wait..." I wasn't fast enough. Sugar cascaded to the floor and the container followed, propelled by Lester's elbow as he tried to right the sugar bag.

I'VE NEVER THOUGHT OF measuring rooms for an appraisal as restful. Now I looked forward to the work. George had come in about ten-thirty and repeated some of the instructions. What he said made more sense now that I'd spent time using, or trying to use, the equipment. I still didn't get the cappuccino machine, but Lester seemed to.

I had to get to the house I was visiting at exactly eleven o'clock. Mrs. Hardy--that's missus, not miz--had retired last year from her job as a waitress in Newhart's Diner. On the phone she had explained that now that her time was her own, she had a schedule for everything, even grocery shopping. My guess was her schedule was how she felt busy.

Mrs. Hardy's house was on E Street, but about a mile south of Mr. Markle's store. The house had two units. She lived in one and had a tenant in the upstairs apartment, which was reached via an external staircase. Mrs. Hardy and her late husband had bought a one-story house forty years ago and added the upstairs. She would get enough from the sale to be served in a good restaurant every day for the rest of her life. And then some.

I walked into the first-floor kitchen where Mrs. Hardy was drinking a cup of spiced tea. It didn't smell good to me.

"Is this a good time for you to take me upstairs?"

She took a key from a row of hooks near the door that separated her kitchen and living room. As we walked up the exterior staircase, she said, "My tenant's been away for several days, so you'll see a pile of mail on the kitchen counter."

"I'll need to take pictures. I can move the pile elsewhere and then put it back where you had it."

Unlike the downstairs, Mrs. Hardy walked from room to room with me. I assumed she wanted to ensure that her tenant's things were not disturbed.

I stretched my tape measure across the bedroom, and then went to the kitchen. "Do you think your tenant will want to stay after you sell it? Sometimes that helps secure a sale."

She hesitated. "He might want to, but he can't. I like Joe Regan, but I've told him to leave by the first of the month. I can't have a person here if somebody wants to shoot them."

I dropped my notebook and stooped to retrieve it. "Gee. I'm, uh, sorry for both of you."

She sighed as she watched me move the mail to the table in the dining area. "It's my daughter, really. She says I won't be safe. A friend of hers has asked me to sell it to her on several occasions. I don't think she even needs financing."

"So, I'm here so you know what to charge her?"

"Yes." She did a more dramatic sigh. "I'll give her a discount, since I won't need to pay realtor fees."

My mind raced as I took photos. The apartment didn't look as if anyone had searched it. If Joe had something valuable that someone else wanted, he would be crazy to leave it in an obvious place in his apartment. *If he has something he shouldn't. You don't know that he does.*

I couldn't snoop in a house I was appraising. Even if Mrs. Hardy asked me to, it would be unethical. I wouldn't. But maybe George...

"You certainly are thorough. Why did you take three pictures of the cabinets above the sink?"

I'd been daydreaming. "I wasn't sure the lighting was right. With digital cameras it's easier to take a few shots rather than look at them before I decide to take another."

Mrs. Hardy shook her head. "Everything's so different."

I had finished interior photos and put my camera in my purse so I could move the mail back to the counter. The two piles I'd neatly arranged sort of fell into each other as I started to pick them up.

"Lazy man's load," Mrs. Hardy said.

"Riiight." In the middle of the muddled mail was an index card with a note in block print. It must have been slipped into the mailbox that sat by the street, and she hadn't noticed it. *Mrs. Hardy's daughter really would like this*. In bold letters, it said, "You're dead."

JAVA JOLT HAD three customers, all of whom had been served, when I walked in. George was showing Talbot Peters the price list taped to the cash register. It had been Lester's and my cheat sheet, so we didn't have to look at the large price board on the wall behind us every time someone paid.

"Hey, Jolie. Sorry I couldn't come for training, but I did learn to pronounce your name." Talbot had on a Java Jolt apron over a pair of brown dress slacks.

He'll have coffee or hot chocolate on those in an hour. "Like we say at Harvest for All, volunteers rock."

George looked surprised to see me. As I left to appraise Mrs. Hardy's house, I'd said I might move to Alaska before I did another shift at Java Jolt. "Jolie. Did you want to go over the cappuccino machine again?"

I started to blurt what I'd found, but stopped. Joe might know Talbot Peters, but he would not appreciate Talbot knowing there was a death threat in his apartment. *Nuts, I meant to tell Joe Talbot was going to help.* "You'll be here tomorrow right, George? You can show me then."

"You feel okay?" George asked.

I was tired. I'm not usually up at six AM. "Nope." I sat at a table and looked up at the two men, who stood behind the counter. "The house I just appraised was a duplex. Joe lives upstairs. Wonder if he'll be able to climb steps well?"

"It's his arm that's hurt," George said. "And if he needs to stay somewhere, it's not my house." He turned back to the register and finished showing Talbot something.

George came to the customer side and sat with me, his expression questioning. He said, "We're lucky. Talbot is a whiz with the register."

I smiled at Talbot who looked as if he'd be more comfortable if George were still instructing him. I looked back to George. "Can we step outside? I need to talk to you about something about Aunt Madge."

He stood up. "Of course."

"I can go to the back," Talbot said.

I smiled. "Nothing personal, Talbot. Just family stuff."

"Of course." He returned the grin, showing his white teeth and violet eyes to full advantage.

A voice from the back table asked, "Is Madge okay?"

Nuts. It was a woman who used to teach Sunday School at First Prez. "She's okay. No worries."

When George and I got outside I walked a few meters and stood in front of the building next to Java Jolt. "That'll start rumors."

"Jolie, what the hell? Is your aunt okay?"

"Yes. But we can't talk about what I'm going to tell you to anyone but Scoobie." I outlined Joe's upcoming eviction and the note in the pile of mail.

George actually whistled. "Did you see anything he might not want you to see?"

I shook my head. "And I really can't look. It didn't seem anyone else had been there searching."

"You mean you don't have a key?" George asked.

"I often don't, people let me in. But that's not the point. It wouldn't be ethical."

He rolled his eyes. "If you really wanted to..."

The First Prez Sunday School teacher stuck her head out of Java Jolt. "Jolie?"

George and I walked toward her. "Really, Aunt Madge is fine," I said.

"I just need a refill," she said, holding up her mug.

CHAPTER ELEVEN

TALBOT PETERS MUST have gone out the back door almost as soon as George and I walked out to the boardwalk. We'd talked about whether someone we didn't know well should have access to the cash register, but George and Scoobie and I thought one of us would be with him at all times. However, nothing was taken. Not even the cash from the honor sugar bowl.

Several customers came in as I was refilling the Sunday School teacher's cup. *Why can't I remember names better?*

George checked the bathroom to be sure Talbot was not in there on the floor. Nope.

Half an hour later it grew quieter again and I knew how to work the cappuccino machine. I had intended to call Morehouse ASAP to tell him about the note, but the customer rush had delayed me.

I walked out to the boardwalk to make the call. It was so quiet I could hear the waves breaking, even though it was low tide. It would have been a peaceful fall day if the seagulls weren't squawking over which one got to sit on the top of a bench a couple stores down.

Just before I pushed the send button for Morehouse's

mobile number, Talbot Peters' face came into my mind. He had the questioning expression he'd worn when standing by the cash register as George and I sat in front of him. *Damn.* I thought I knew who put that note in Joe's pile of mail.

I walked back into Java Jolt and looked at the clock above the coffee machines. Three-thirty. Scoobie would be done working by now. He said he would come to the shop when he got off, since it was the first day "you novices are operating it." When Scoobie got to Java Jolt, I'd think of a reason to get back into Mrs. Hardy's upstairs apartment. If my instincts were right, the note would already be gone.

George tilted his head by way of asking me to join him behind the counter. In a low voice, he said, "I had him hang his jacket on one of those pegs by the back door. It's gone."

"Somehow, I think he was here to look for something, not do a favor for Joe."

"I asked if I could do a reference check," George said. "I apologized, but he said he understood we didn't know him, and that I couldn't get in touch with Joe right then."

"Who did he have you call?" I asked.

"Some guy named Mike who works at Trenton City Hall. I have the number in the back."

"Did this Mike answer the phone himself?"

"Yeah." George ran fingers through his hair. "Coulda been anyone answering. Even Peters himself."

"Listen, George, I want to go look at that note again. Tell Scoobie about it, but not that I've gone back there, okay?"

He narrowed his eyes. "Why?"

"Because I want to be sure it's still there."

George's expression changed from puzzlement to realization. "Crud."

Scoobie came in, looked at me, and said, "You look like you need a nap."

"I'll grab one before I go finish planning the costume donation and giveaway thing with Megan this evening." I looked at George. "Catch you guys later."

"What?" Scoobie asked, looking between George and me.

I yawned. "George'll tell you about Talbot. We can talk tonight, okay?"

Scoobie nodded and kissed me on the cheek. I made it out of there just as a group of teachers came in for after-school voltage.

MRS. HARDY WAS surprised to see me.

"I should have looked at those pictures a few times as I took them. May I go back up to take a couple more photos in the kitchen?"

She looked as if I was trying her patience.

I smiled, I hoped in an engaging way. "If you don't want to climb the steps, I can be up and down in a jiffy."

"Come in." She walked back to her kitchen and returned with the key. "If I can't trust Madge Richards' niece, who can I trust?"

Gulp.

If I hadn't been so tired I'd have jogged up the outside staircase to the second level. Sure enough, the mail was spread out on the kitchen counter, as if someone had gone through it. The death threat was gone.

Discouraged, I walked back down the steps. Why hadn't I thought to go to the house as soon as we knew Talbot had left Java Jolt? Or maybe the disappearing note had been a good thing. We could be sure someone was angry with Joe.

Crud. Before heading home I stopped at Harvest for All. I hoped Megan would be there and we could have our costume logistics discussion so I didn't have to go out again tonight. She was not, but Connie was talking animatedly to Monica, who seemed her usual half-befuddled self.

The door dinged as I walked in. "Hello Connie. Nice to see you."

She gave me her engaging smile. "I appreciate all you've done for me. I wanted to volunteer some."

It no longer surprises me that people who have little are the most likely to give to others. "That would be fabulous. Megan usually does a volunteer training session on Friday afternoons. It's short."

She looked disappointed. "Oh, I guess I can wait." She brightened. "Unless you could do it now. I could help you stock shelves or something." Her eyes roamed the pantry.

"Hmm. We ought to wait for Megan. She likes to get everyone started the same way. She knows a lot more about the customer work than I do." In reality, I probably know as much, but we like to establish that Megan is the formal supervisor. I've even talked her into taking twenty-five dollars a week, which comes out to about two dollars an hour. We call it an honorarium.

"Oh, okay. I'll come back Friday."

"One o'clock," I said. "And thank you."

Connie left, and Monica turned to me. "I didn't realize you knew her. I was being a bit stand-offish because I hadn't seen her before."

"Mary Margaret brought it but it's good to be cautious when we don't know someone well. I think we have her information somewhere. She was going to bring in a

Medicaid card so we'd know she's eligible for regular service."

"Good," Monica said, straightening her cardigan. "I get tongue tied when I try to give instructions."

That explains the confusion at the bake sale tables.

I PULLED INTO the gravel drive and sat looking at my house. Scoobie and I had intended to paint the porch railings this past summer. That seemed trivial right now.

My mind saw the mail in Joe's apartment. Before neatening it I had taken a couple of photos of the letters littering the table. The Nancy Drew part of my mind thought maybe we could tell something about when the note had been left by where it was placed in the pile. The logical portion told me to get real.

Talbot Peters was the only explanation for the theft. How on earth could he have gotten up there? Glumly, I thought he probably had special skills with a credit card or some kind of fancy lock pick.

Nuts! I remembered Mrs. Hardy had a hearing aid in at least one ear. In summer there would be lots of people around to notice a stranger on Mrs. Hardy's exterior staircase. Since a man usually lived up there, and Talbot had a similar build to Joe's, the few people around at this time of year would not have given Talbot a second thought.

I turned off the ignition, got out of the car, and walked onto the porch. When I opened the door, Jazz bolted out. "Jazz! Jazz!" I looked toward traffic in the street and stifled a scream.

A car swerved to avoid her and Jazz made it across Bayside Street. Barely. I couldn't run as fast as she could, but

Ground to a Halt

I made time pretty quickly. Straight across from where she had crossed was the open gate to Charlotte Evans' back yard.

I ran into the yard and looked around. Very few houses near the beach have manicured lawns. It's sandy soil, at best. The Evans are wealthy. What I could see of the back yard looked like a botanical garden. I didn't know the names of any plants except the roses. *So many places to hide.*

The back door opened and I recognized Charlotte's voice. "Jolie, I think your cat ran back there." She pointed to the back of the lawn, left corner.

My voice caught. "She's never run out like that."

"Something must have scared her." Charlotte walked off the porch. As I went toward the back of the small yard she shut the gate so Jazz couldn't run out.

"Thanks," I called back to her. I got to the four-inch tall line of bricks in front of the plants and stooped. "Jazz?"

She meowed, and I almost cried. "Come out, baby."

It sounded as if she was behind the largest rose bush, which was surrounded by what remained of the summer crop of zinnias, whose name I'd just remembered. "Come on." Jazz apparently moved a few inches closer, as I could see her green eyes.

I tapped the bricks, hoping she would think it was a game. She meowed more loudly, but didn't budge. I didn't feel like getting scratched by a bunch of thorns.

Charlotte was behind me, every bit her perfectly coiffed self. "Walk to the gate with me. She'll think you're leaving and come to you."

I stood, not wanting to do as she suggested, but not about to contradict her when my cat was in her garden.

"Come on. Talk normally, as if you've forgotten all about

her. I'll start. It was nice of you and your friends to operate Java Jolt for Joe."

"Oh, it should work out." After we'd gone a few steps I turned my head. Jazz was sitting on the bricks. I patted my thigh, something Scoobie does when he wants Jazz or the dogs to pay attention to him. She trotted to me.

I picked her up and sobbed once. "Why did you run?"

Charlotte put a hand on my shoulder. "The idea of losing a pet is unbearable."

I looked at her as I sort of slung Jazz to my shoulder. "Thanks so much. So silly.."

"Not at all."

I walked across the street, rubbing Jazz under her chin. She wanted to get down and I was trying to distract her. When we got to the front door it was all I could do to keep a grip on her. I opened the storm door and pushed the main door open with my foot.

I gasped. "No wonder." I had the presence of mind to pull the storm door shut just as Jazz jumped down.

Whoever had searched the house had been thorough. The cushions on the rocker were slashed and someone had picked up the small area rug and tossed it a few feet from where it usually sat. The couch cushions were on the floor but not slashed.

I stood in the doorway and called a familiar number. Morehouse picked up on the third ring. "What, Jolie?"

"I...I should have called 9-1-1."

AUNT MADGE PULLED UP at the same time as the police cruiser. I was on my porch swing. I'd left Jazz in the house. She had tried to come out with me, but I didn't think I could hold onto her long enough to get her into my car, so I swung my foot in her direction and she backed up. I'm pretty sure she gave me a dirty look.

Two male officers who looked like high school students ran toward me, but Aunt Madge beat them. She's the fastest eighty-plus woman in New Jersey.

"Someone in there now?" the taller one asked.

I shook my head. "I'm pretty sure no, but I didn't look."

They walked into the house the way police do on TV, guns straight in front of them, yelling "clear" as they moved from room to room. I had a brief sense of dread. *What if they get shot going through our house?*

Aunt Madge had sat next to me on the swing at some point. I hadn't even noticed. She put an arm around my shoulder. "I thought all that happened was you almost lost Jazz. Are you hurt? Charlotte said you were about to cry."

I shook my head and turned teary eyes to her. "Jazz got out. She could have been killed."

"You got her though." Her tone was designed to soothe me, and it helped a bit.

I nodded at my front door. "I put her down when I walked in. I made her stay when I came back out. She'll be under the bed with Pebbles until people leave."

Charlotte Evans came to her front door and waved. Aunt Madge waved back and then turned her attention back to me. "She called as you were leaving her yard. When she said you were crying I hopped in the car."

I looked at her clearly. She still wore the apron she uses to bake afternoon bread for her guests. Today her hair was dark blonde. She uses temporary color and changes it every month or so. I smiled, still teary. "I'd like to see you hop."

The shorter officer came out to the porch. His brown hair curled so tightly it looked like a perm. "No one there, but we'd like you to stay out here until one of the senior officers arrives." He walked off the porch toward his police cruiser.

The other patrol officer opened the front door and leaned out. "Is that a skunk under the bed with the cat?"

"Yes, but she's more scared of you than vice versa," I said.

"And she doesn't spray," Aunt Madge added.

Morehouse's car pulled up. The patrol officer near the cars talked quietly to him, and Morehouse came over to Aunt Madge and me. "What the hell is this about, Jolie?"

I burst into tears and he actually stepped back a foot. "How would I know? Why does, does stuff always happen to *me*?"

I WOKE UP ON the bed in my old room at the Cozy Corner. Someone had called an ambulance, but I refused to go to the hospital. If Morehouse had had a sedative he would have forced it in me, but I said I didn't want anything, only to be away. When I said I didn't care if anything was taken, he realized I wouldn't be any help and let me leave with Aunt Madge.

It was comforting to see the familiar antique furniture, minus the rocker, which Aunt Madge had given me as a housewarming present. The meow from the bottom of the bed meant Jazz was at the B&B with me. I didn't remember bringing her. *Maybe Scoobie is here.*

The door opened and he peered in. "Decent nap. Next time you should probably crash at Java Jolt." His attempt at humor pretty much failed.

I took in his expression, which now included a frown. Not his usual countenance, but we don't get our house broken into every day. Jazz sailed off the bed and into the hallway. That did make me smile. "I bet the dogs were glad to see her."

I sat up and Scoobie sat on the bed next to me. "Yeah, Mr. Rogers didn't even mind when she jumped on his back and, you won't believe this, Miss Piggy tried to give Jazz a bone."

"Is the house okay?"

"They didn't do much in the bedrooms. Morehouse said to leave cushions on the floor and drawers and stuff open in the kitchen. He wants you to see if anything is missing."

"Our computers? They were in the bedrooms, right?"

"Fine. Yours was on the chair in front of the desk. Looked as if they were trying to get it unattached from the printer when you came home."

"Wow, I guess they went out the back. Did the police take mine?"

He nodded. "Dust for prints. I told them they could take it, but they aren't going to check your files until they talk to you. I think they need your permission."

"I'm not letting them check my files," I huffed, and then sighed. "Now we *really* know Joe is hiding something from us."

"Or someone thinks that," Scoobie said. "I heard Morehouse tell Dana to make sure Joe was still at the hospital."

"Hey." I sat up. "How'd they get in?"

"I know I didn't leave it unlocked, you didn't right?" When I shook my head, he said, "Lock picks, maybe."

"That makes me feel really safe." *Not!*

"The first thing out of George's mouth was he bet we

didn't have the security system on." Scoobie gave me a questioning look and I nodded.

George bought the system for me last year after Aunt Madge reamed him out for an article she thought made me less safe at home. I didn't like the article either, but I liked the system. *Why don't I set that every day?*

"I need to go make Joe say who hates him enough to come after me." I started to get out of bed and Scoobie put a hand on my shoulder to keep me seated.

"You can get in line tomorrow." He frowned. "He won't go anywhere. Madge already invited him to stay here for a couple of days. Harry's picking him up at the hospital tomorrow."

That's great. Someone may want to kill Joe and he'll be staying here. "Umm. There's something we need to talk about. Maybe you, me, and George."

Scoobie looked at me with suspicion. "What did you do?"

"I hate it when people ask me that!"

Scoobie raised his eyebrows.

"I'm sorry I snapped."

"Okay, you get a pass today." He squeezed my knee. "What is it?"

"Okay, George told you about the note when you got to Java Jolt."

"Yeah, and I don't like it, but it's not our business."

By the time I finished telling him the note was gone and I thought Talbot Peters might have taken it, Scoobie was reaching into his pocket for his mobile phone.

"Are you calling George?"

Scoobie almost snorted. "The police. They…"

"Can you wait one minute?"

"Why?"

"I guess I'd like to talk to Joe about…" When Scoobie looked about to disagree, I touched his arm and continued. "There's nothing for them to find now. Think how upset Mrs. Hardy will be if the police show up at this time of night."

Scoobie considered that. "Okay. No sense waking her up."

Now, if he can forget about it later…

CHAPTER TWELVE

AUNT MADGE'S IMPECCABLE grapevine had informed her Mrs. Hardy would not renew Joe's lease. She didn't know Joe well, but told me she thought he needed a couple of days to get used to having an arm in a sling before he had to look for a new place.

Sometimes she surprises even me. Because I was beginning to think that Joe Regan really was involved in something shady, I didn't like this surprise. I debated confiding my concerns to Aunt Madge.

She's a smart woman, she must have considered everything that happened. But her mind isn't as suspicious as mine is.

I was sitting at the table in Aunt Madge's kitchen, across from Joe. "I swear to God, Jolie, it can't have anything to do with me. I'm not some kind of…some kind of crook who hides money or something with people I barely know."

I tried to keep my temper reigned in. This was helped because the fingers that stuck out of Joe's cast were swollen and he looked like death on a cracker. He had touched up his roots, so his hair was all auburn again. *How do you do that in a hospital? Shoe polish?*

"I don't think you hid money or something with me, if that's what you mean. But someone seems to think you did."

Joe thought for a moment. "I had a pretty rough life in Kansas right before I came east. It was the recession, remember? I bunked with friends or friends of friends. For all I know, one of them could be someone who stole money and someone thinks I ended up with it." He gently massaged his swollen fingers.

"I've never thought of you as some kind of robber on the run. It's just the only thing different in my life is seeing you right after you got shot."

"That was a pretty bad day for me, too."

"Think. Was there anyone in Kansas who might believe you had something of theirs? Something worth not just finding you at Java Jolt but breaking into my house, too?"

Joe shook his head, slowly. "I bunked where I could the last six months I was in Kansas. A couple of the guys I didn't know well. Kind of rough backgrounds, one was proud of a couple of prison tattoos. Met them in the unemployment line."

"So, maybe someone's really looking for them, or maybe…"

Joe's smile was grim. "Your imagination's gotten you in trouble before. It...hey. Do you know when that robbery was that the police are talking about?"

"You don't?" I asked.

"I *wasn't* there."

I told him the dates that were in the Kansas paper, and his face lit up.

He grinned. "I was already gone! See, I told you I didn't know those people."

How can he prove that? "You should tell Sergeant Morehouse that, if you haven't already."

"I will. I was so woozy in the hospital I never asked him about the exact dates." He sat up straighter, looking excited. "You found some kind of jewelry in your place when you moved in. When Scoobie was helping you paint or something. Maybe somebody's looking for it. That's who searched your house!"

"It's still in police evidence and I'm still trying to find who owned it."

"I bet it was that," he insisted.

"I really want to believe you."

He stared at my impassive expression for a second. "You don't think it was me who broke in, do you?"

"Not unless you have a third arm."

"Plus, Harry didn't bring me to Ocean Alley until this morning." He grinned for second. "I can't believe your aunt."

I studied his earnest face, and sighed. "We all appreciate what you do for Harvest for All. But there is something you need to know, and you might not want…"

Aunt Madge walked into the kitchen. "Jolie, let the poor man rest."

"Oh, sure, you're right." *Thank goodness she didn't hear me say he might not want Aunt Madge to hear.* I stood. "I'll catch the poor man later." It wasn't as if I had the death threat to show him.

WHEN I GOT to my house police tape across the top step on the porch stopped me. Scoobie didn't go there before work, he had brought his scrubs to the Cozy Corner. Still, police tape had not occurred to me.

I dialed the main police station number, hoping to get Dana. I lucked out.

She listened to the request to enter my house, and said she needed to check on something. When she returned to the phone, she said, "We're done in there, and Scoobie set the alarm last night. Just pull the tape down. Call if anything looks out of place."

"Besides the stuffing from the rocking chair pillows?"

"At least it wasn't your couch cushions." She hung up without saying goodbye.

She's getting more like Morehouse.

The tape was easy to pull down, and I remembered the alarm code before it gave its warning buzz. That was the easy part. Whoever had searched was messy, but not completely destructive. He, or she, had pulled the lamp table away from the wall to look behind it, but though the lamp shade was crooked the picture frames were still standing.

Couch cushions were tossed around, but they had zippers in the back. The searcher had opened them and found nothing. I picked the cushions off the floor, redid the zippers, and put them back on the couch.

I don't have a lot of possessions. When the condo my ex-husband and I owned in Lakewood was sold to pay back some of the money he embezzled from his employer, we left most furniture in it. Scoobie's books are in neatly stacked tubs on one wall in the guest bedroom, and they had not been disturbed. I hoped no one came back to search them. *I wonder how much a baby cam monitor costs?*

By later today I wanted to have the house cleaned up and be able to explain to Scoobie that there was no reason to tell the police about the death note, as I had mentally dubbed it.

Its removal made it kind of useless information. More important, I didn't want Mrs. Hardy to find out that I lied about needing another photo. Plus, I would have lied while doing appraisal work. Bad for Harry's business. Maybe I could get Scoobie to agree it was pointless to pass on the note's existence or my theory that Talbot Peters took it.

I peered under our bed, and Pebbles eyed me, not moving. "Come on out. You know it's me." She didn't move, so I stood and examined my closet. It didn't look as if anyone had even parted the hangers of clothes.

Two of the kitchen drawers sat on the floor, their contents dumped on the small kitchen table. I replaced them both in their slots and began putting utensils and silverware back in them. *Morehouse really needs to tell me the name of the guy whose fingerprints were on the Java Jolt door.*

The rocker cushions went into a black trash bag and I scrubbed a small amount of fingerprint dust from the kitchen counter and around the front doorknob. My guess would be that the police decided the intruder wore gloves and stopped checking for more prints.

A soft patter announced Pebbles, and she walked to the fridge and stood next to it, expectations clear.

"You want some fresh veggies?"

No response, so I crumbled a few pieces of cauliflower, put it in her food bowl, and refilled her water bowl. "No one took you, I see." She ignored me. "I'll bring Jazz back this afternoon." Pebbles looked at me and went back to munching. I have no idea if a skunk learns any words. She certainly hasn't responded to Scoobie's instructions to roll over, but I don't think he's serious about it.

My phone chirped and I glanced at caller ID. "Good morning, Sergeant."

"Anything missin'?"

"Doesn't seem to be. You know who it was?"

"No prints. You can stop by and get your computer."

"Wouldn't it be nice if you told me whose prints were at the coffee shop the day Joe got shot?"

"How in the hell do you know about that?"

Nuts. I improvised. "Joe, but he didn't remember the name."

"You don't have a need to know."

"Okay. Were the prints anywhere else?"

"Where any prints were is not your…"

"I mean were they on business doors besides Java Jolt? You know, as if a robber was checking a bunch of stores."

Morehouse didn't say anything for a moment. Then he went with his usual. "I told you to keep your nose out of this." He hung up.

I glanced at the phone before sticking it in my pocket. "You wouldn't say that if your house got broken into."

WHEN IN DOUBT, I go to the library. I had never tried on my own to find out about the person whose fingerprints were on the Java Jolt door the day Joe was shot. My guess was the bank robber from Kansas.

I could have done Google searches at home but, again, didn't want Scoobie to know what I was doing. *If he asks if I've searched for information on an old bank robbery, I'll tell him the truth.* Not that I expected him to ask.

I also was more certain than ever that I hadn't gotten the truth from Joe Regan. Someone thought he had hidden something in my house. He had something hidden somewhere, or I wouldn't be about to shop for rocker cushions.

Why me? Maybe because you visited him in the hospital. Twice. Did someone follow me? Not likely, though I hadn't paid any attention to traffic behind me. It could be as simple as I'd been in Java Jolt the morning Joe was shot, and I was near him on the sidewalk immediately after he was hurt. *Nuts.*

For forty-five minutes I searched for Kansas bank robberies for the time period four to five years ago. There were some, and there were follow-up articles on a couple of trials and several sentencing hearings.

Nothing looked right. It appeared most crimes were solved or had suspects, though a couple didn't. I reminded myself that the guy who'd been at Java Jolt had gotten out of prison, so he'd obviously been arrested. Whoever he was.

I was about to give up when I did one last search with every relevant word I could think of. I used no quotation marks around a phrase, so words did not have to appear together to come up in the search. I keyed in, Kansas, bank robbery, four five years ago, three-year sentence, and parole. It was mumbo jumbo, but the first item in the results was "Belken Surfaces in New Jersey."

Why hadn't I thought of current articles? I peered at the computer and read.

> Barry Belken, who robbed the Four Squares Credit Union in Kansas City, Missouri, nearly five years ago, has resurfaced in New Jersey. Belken was released on parole four months ago, but after

checking in with his parole officer twice he failed to appear for more visits.

When New Jersey police investigated an apparent burglary, Belken's fingerprints were found on the exterior door of a coffee shop in Ocean Alley. There was no sign of him. The coffee shop is operated by Joe Regan, a former Kansas resident who told police that he never knew Belken. Regan was never considered a suspect in the Four Squares robbery, and has no criminal history.

At the time of his arrest, only hours after Four Squares was robbed, Belken had no money in his possession and would not confess to the crime. He always maintained that, despite security camera photos, his arrest was a case of mistaken identity. He never named the man police believe had intended to drive the getaway car. When police, summoned by a silent alarm, neared the credit union, a black SUV, later determined to be stolen, pulled away from the curb in front of Four Squares. Belken left on foot, from the bank's alley entrance.

Kansas City Police speculate that Belken either wants to hide with someone he knew prior to the robbery, or is looking for the cash he stole. He may be in the company of a former girlfriend, Benji Radin. Radin has a record of petty theft, but no arrests since Belken went to prison. She has not been seen since Belken violated his parole, and police believe he may be forcing her to remain with him.

Not long after Belken apparently broke into the coffee shop, owner Joe Regan was seriously wounded in an attack in broad daylight in Ocean Alley. Regan, who is recovering, could not identify his attacker.

Kansas City Police have issued a warrant for Belken's arrest and distributed that information to state and local law enforcement as well as the FBI.

So, the robbery had been in Missouri, that's why I had trouble finding it. "Damn." I looked around to see if my comment had disturbed anyone. Morehouse told a newspaper in Kansas about the prints, but he wouldn't tell me whose they were. *Jerk*.

Armed with his name, I searched for Barry Belken and almost immediately found a couple of articles on the robbery from about five years ago. A link to a video, had apparently been taken down. Unfortunately, the articles provided little additional information.

The only photo was of a man with a thin face, straggly hair, a short goatee, and handlebar mustache. It was not a good look. Especially since his green eyes were glaring at the camera.

How can I use this information? That would take some figuring. Scoobie would be annoyed that I was digging into a robbery Joe might or might not be connected to. George said he wouldn't keep information from Scoobie. I knew there could be some temporary wiggle room there, but ultimately George would want to stay on his best friend's good side.

I love Scoobie. But why does he have to be so uninterested in unanswered questions?

CHAPTER THIRTEEN

FORTUNATELY, HARVEST FOR ALL has more responsible volunteers than I. Megan and Aretha had finalized plans for the costume drop-off and giveaway without me. I had gotten the *Ocean Alley Press* and radio stations to agree to publicize that we wanted children's costumes. We even have a Facebook page now, thanks to Daphne. Librarians think of everything.

I'm not an after-the-fact critic, but I was a little concerned that we had decided to do the drop-off and giveaway the same day. The donations were to come in during the daytime, and the giveaway would start at four in the afternoon, as kids were getting home from school. Aretha was probably right -- it would be easier for us to get volunteers on one day instead of two or three. We'd keep costumes on hand until Halloween, so stragglers could get them other days.

It was only a few days before the fundraiser. Our planning was really compressed. However, because we had the generous services of the country club, there was no need to hustle for food to feed attendees or volunteers to manage a lot of games. Kids know how to trick-or-treat, and they expect candy at a Halloween party, not action. Or so I hoped.

In any event, today I stood at the counter at Harvest for all accepting non-perishable food and costumes that sported spiders and what looked like zombie blood.

It didn't take long to realize that half of the families in Ocean Alley wanted to get rid of costumes that had taken up space in closets or trunks for years. A tall woman sporting a black sweatshirt with orange pumpkins brought in an armload of pastel-colored fabric. It turned out to be half a dozen princess outfits, in varied sizes.

"I didn't want to give these away, but my daughter has three boys and she says she's done being pregnant." She looked at the pile of costumes and sighed. "No sense hanging onto these."

I offered her a donation receipt, which she declined, and carried the clothes into the First Prez hallway that abuts the pantry. Sylvia had brought into the hall the rolling racks used to hold coats during Sunday services. "We need more hangers," she said, looking stressed. For her that meant her shoulders weren't ramrod straight.

"Scoobie's going to call when he gets done at the hospital just after three. He can stop and buy a few batches of wire coat hangers. They're cheap."

Aunt Madge was seated at a portable sewing machine in the conference room where we have committee meetings. She has a fancy one at the Cozy Corner, , but transporting it would be a big deal. Harry had carried in the small machine, saying that he had bought it used yesterday and oiled it up. "Madge said there will be costumes with rips and tears. You won't want to give kids stuff that doesn't look good."

I looked into the conference room. Aunt Madge's hair was orange today, with a streak of black from her forehead to the nape of her neck. "Thank you, Aunt Madge."

She stopped sewing and looked up. "I see a future weekend in Maryland with Harry's family, with you minding the Cozy Corner."

"Everyone's a clairvoyant near Halloween." I grinned, gave her a four-fingered wave, and started back to the pantry.

I had done two appraisal visits yesterday and one this morning, and even managed to get all the floor plan measurements in the computer. I envisioned a long day in the courthouse tomorrow to check for comps. I couldn't have a better boss. Another one would tell me to work my Harvest for All schedule around appraisals and not vice versa.

It wasn't long before I decided we needed those hangers well before three and dashed to Wal Mart and back. I was feverishly hanging costumes on the clothes racks when Lester announced himself. I glanced at the doorway and felt faint with apprehension. *We'll scare away the donors.*

Lester was dressed in the pirate costume he'd used at our Talk Like a Pirate Day fundraiser a few years ago. He looked like a worker pirate ready to swab a deck. He wore a sleeveless white tee-shirt, knee-length cut-off jeans, and a bandana around his head. A large pipe dangled from his mouth in place of the customary unlit cigar. He had a canvas sack slung over his shoulder and a huge grin on his face. "So, whaddya think?"

I was pretty sure Sylvia gagged, but I beat her to a comment.

"Very authentic, Lester. But, uh, why today and not the party in a few days?"

He looked a bit uncomfortable. "The dirt bag head waiter at the club doesn't always wanna let me in."

"Imagine that," Sylvia said. Until she spoke I thought she

might have frozen with a skeleton costume over her arm.

Lester gave her what he probably thought was a disarming smile but looked more like a leer. "It wasn't my fault."

I didn't bother to ask what wasn't. Instead, I said, "Maybe you can help go through the donated costumes to see if any need to be repaired."

He waved a long rubber sword. "Aye, aye, matey." He followed the whirr of Aunt Madge's sewing machine and walked into the hall.

Megan was behind Sylvia, trying to look busy so she didn't laugh too hard. Sylvia looked at me. "I wonder if we've got too many crab pots in the water?"

I wanted to say if she was worried I was leaving, but settled for, "No, just enthusiastic crabbers."

Scoobie came in about three-thirty. He was dressed in black jeans and a black tee shirt, with a skeleton mask on his head, ready to be pulled over his face. *Why is it that guys always wear scary costumes?*

Sylvia had gone to the church office to have a cup of coffee, so I put Scoobie in charge of ensuring the costumes were organized by size.

He looked at the rack. "Are you separating by boys' and girls' costumes?"

He was greeted by brief stares from Aretha, Megan, Daphne and me.

"I think you're supposed to think most of them are gender-neutral," Lance said. He had arrived a few minutes earlier, bearing a bag of donuts and Max.

Scoobie didn't miss a beat. "If you want to wear a tu-tu it's fine with me."

Megan tossed an apple at him.

"Scoobie, boys don't..." Max began.

"Joke, Max. Remember we talked about how not all humor is straight-out funny?"

Max thought for a moment. "Now I get what you meant." He took an apple from the counter. "But I don't want a tu-tu."

WHEN WE SHUT THE DOORS at seven o'clock, Lance, Max, Scoobie, and I sat or sprawled around the conference room. Others had left in stages, based on when they had to cook dinner or pick up someone from work. Thankfully, Lester was scheduled to show a home at five-thirty. I didn't think he would have had time to change, but it wasn't my business.

I looked up at Lance from my spot on the floor. "How many left?"

"I'd say fifteen or twenty, varied sizes." He glanced at Scoobie. "No tu-tus."

"Dang," Scoobie said.

I stared at the ceiling. "We'll probably get more donations over the next couple of days. And more people wanting them."

"How is your foot, your foot, Jolie?" Max asked.

"It's okay. The baby in the stroller wasn't heavy." I wiggled my toes, thankful I'd had on sneakers and not a more flimsy pair of shoes. In her confusion after I yelped, the mom had rolled the stroller backwards so it had gone over my foot twice.

"Lance, you want to go to Newhart's Diner with Scoobie, Max, and me?"

"Only if Scoobie wears his mask."

SLEEP EVADED ME, so I listened to Scoobie's gentle breathing and moved closer to him. It wouldn't be fair to wake him, since he had to get up early to go to work.

Scoobie's even breathing had almost lulled me to sleep when my eyes flew open. Two things happened the day Joe got shot and both of them were near Mr. Markle's store. Morehouse had told me he initially went to Java Jolt in casual clothes because police were investigating a car accident. Later, Mr. Markle said one person had fled the accident scene. *What if that person was the same one who later shot Joe?*

CHAPTER FOURTEEN

THE NEXT MORNING, MY BRAIN was still in a fog from Joe's shooting and the mess at our bungalow. If it hadn't been for someone trashing our house, I think I could have let go of the shooting. What Joe had done or not done in his past had nothing to do with me. Scoobie and I, with others, could keep track of Max to be sure no one bothered him, and Joe could be on his own.

But, some pure dirt bag, to use Lester's term, had been in our house, torn up my cushions, and tossed the kitchen. I was angrier than a shark on a fishing line and wanted to know who had the nerve to invade my space. Scoobie's space, too, but he was intent on not worrying about what he couldn't control. That annoys the daylights out of me, but if I tell him he just says serenity takes work.

So, serenity aside, I entered the police station early the next morning. I was supposed to be at Java Jolt by six thirty, but I needed to know who ran away from the car accident. I knew it was too early for Morehouse, but Dana often worked with local schools. She might be at the station.

The officer at the front desk was one of the two who had come to my bungalow after the break-in. His curls were not as tight today, and he did not like my request to see Dana.

"The thing is, she's about to head to the high school to be in the main hallway when the doors open."

"One minute, that's all." I tried to look imploring.

He picked up the phone and pushed two buttons. Someone answered and he told them to ask Corporal Johnson if she could talk to me for a minute. He listened. "In the lobby. Okay." He hung up and looked at me, "Just a sec."

In about five seconds the door that led to the locked area where officers sit opened and Dana came out. "Jolie, what?"

I hadn't wanted to talk where the desk officer could hear but couldn't ask him to put his fingers in his ears. "Remember that accident in front of Mr. Markle's the other day? You know, the day Joe was shot."

She frowned. "I really have to…"

"Who was it who fled that day?"

I could see she was debating her response. "We sent a few sets of prints to Trenton. But I don't think we've heard back yet. A car taken for a joy ride is not a high priority for the lab down there."

"Oh, so not the same person whose prints were on Java Jolt's door?"

She looked from me to the other officer and back to me. "I don't know. I'll check. *Later.* Now I have to get to the high school." She walked out the door that leads to the station's parking lot."

I looked at her back, then at my watch. If I hustled, I'd only be fifteen minutes late to Java Jolt.

IT WAS TWO DAYS before our Saturday Halloween party fundraiser. I finally had my Toyota back, and it seemed mostly repaired. The driver's side window was sluggish, so it would have to go back to the repair shop at some point. There would be time after the fundraiser.

I was in Java Jolt for what I planned to make my last tour of duty. I hadn't minded helping Joe when I thought he was a hapless victim, but I was no longer sure of that. Plus, the constant smell of coffee was bugging my stomach. I only have a couple of cups a day myself, and after being around it so much I wasn't even drinking that much.

The only problem with me cutting back on Java Jolt time was that Max wanted to help George at the shop, and there would not be a good reason to say no. When I explained to Max that it was boring work and sometimes customers were grouchy, he simply said, "Joe helps me. I help Joe." I wish my brain were as clear as his more troubled one can be at times.

"So, Max," I said, "the hot water is only for tea, unless someone wants a bit added to their coffee."

Max regarded me as if I had the brain damage. "Jolie, coffee is mostly water. Water."

"You're right. Sometimes people don't want it to be as strong as we make it. Then they say something like half a cup of coffee and half a cup of water."

"But they pay the same," George added.

"Okay," Max said, "but George takes the money."

From his place at a table on the customer side of the counter, Joe added, "Or I do."

"Or Joe," George amended. "But you won't be here much, right Joe?"

"For now," Joe said.

George began showing Max where the paper cups and napkins were stored, and I made myself a cup of peppermint tea and went to Joe's table. The only other people in the shop were two local couples, and if they wanted refills, they would likely get them from the thermoses on the counter.

"Aunt Madge treating you okay?"

Joe nodded. "When I let her. I have to keep reminding her not to ask me if I want anything."

"Ah, good. You must be feeling better."

"Getting there. I do appreciate not having to cook meals. I'll have to load up on frozen dinners before I go…wherever."

I glanced toward the counter to be sure Max and George weren't listening. "I'm sorry you have to find a new place to live."

"How did you know that?"

"Mrs. Hardy had me do an appraisal." I wished I hadn't said anything. Joe's look was a mix of anger and pain. "I'm sorry, I shouldn't have said…"

"No, it's okay. I'd been thinking of moving a few more blocks back from the ocean, maybe buying a small place."

"Maybe you'll get a bargain, like I did."

He shrugged, and winced briefly. "Hope to. Probably have to rent for a couple of months. Lester said he'd help me find a place."

"Lucky you."

"Yeah, well, he's been helping here. And you know how…persuasive he can be."

"Don't we all." I had planned a series of questions, and was sorry I had made the comment about Joe's apartment as a lead-in. But, no time like the present. "How did a Kansas boy get from the corn fields to the ocean?"

"Wheat." At my puzzled look, he added, "Corn is Iowa. Wheat is Kansas."

"I can see the grain of truth in that."

He groaned. "You're channeling Scoobie. Not good."

"Sorry. Really, it's quite a switch. I could see going from a factory to running a coffee shop, but why Ocean Alley?"

Joe's quick look at my face and back to his coffee said he was sizing up my intent. "I was only at the ocean once, but it just stayed with me. The freshness, no fertilizer smell, that kind of thing. I couldn't find work in Kansas. When I decided on a change, I came here. I picked Jersey because of Springsteen, if you can believe that."

"Ah. The Asbury Park ideal." Asbury Park is not even ten miles north of Ocean Alley. It's coming back to its glory days, but it'll take awhile. "How did you find the reality?"

His smile was rueful. "Ocean Grove and Ocean Alley are definitely more...upscale. People are friendly here. When I came that first spring, I worked two jobs and slept on the beach, except on the nights the cops rousted me."

"So you could save a lot?"

As he nodded porcelain hit the floor behind us, with a distinct crash.

"I broke it! I broke the cup!" Max called. He and George were toward the back of the shop.

Joe called, "Don't worry about it, Max."

"No worries, no worries," Max repeated.

I didn't hear what George was saying to him, but the tone was one of patience. I looked back at Joe.

"Yeah, had a bit when I got here. Saved a lot. When I got this place it was kind of a dump." He nodded as if encompassing the shop.

"When I lived here in eleventh grade it was part of an arcade. Scoobie and I came here a lot."

"Luckily someone remodeled it for a hot dog and popcorn stand, so the plumbing was redone for a place that sold food. Still took a lot of work."

I studied his face. "And then Hurricane Sandy did a number on it."

"Yeah, but I was luckier than a lot of people. I didn't have huge stoves or walk-in refrigerators like some of the restaurants. Almost all of my equipment could be moved out easily. I just had to gut the place." He looked toward the serving counter. "Came out better."

I nodded. "It did. Listen, Joe, there's one more thing to tell you. It's about your apartment."

"What? Did somebody trash it like your place?"

"No. If it had been searched, the person was a pro. It was your stack of mail…"

"You went through my mail?"

I shook my head. "Of course not. But I had to move it off the counter to take photos for the appraisal. When I moved the mail back I saw a handwritten note. It said, 'You're dead.'"

He looked stunned. "Damn. You have it? Did Mrs. Hardy see it?"

I explained Talbot's abrupt departure and my near-certainty that he had gone to Mrs. Hardy's to get the note."

"Who is Talbot Peters?"

I sighed. "He came by, said he was one of your suppliers and wanted to help. George even did a reference check. But, um, I guess it was a phony reference."

Joe stared at me. "No kidding. What did he look like?"

I described him in detail, adding that his violet eyes would qualify as bedroom eyes in a romance novel.

Though the description seemed to reassure him, Joe had looked a lot better before I told him about the note. But I didn't want to stop asking questions. "You don't think it could have really been Barry Belken, do you?"

Joe looked surprised. "Who is that?"

Is he trying to pull one over on me? "That's the name of the guy whose prints were on the Java Jolt back door the day you got shot." I didn't know this, of course, but wanted to gauge his reaction.

"Do you have a photo of this Belken?" Joe asked.

Damn. I should have printed the photo in the article that was on the library computer. I shook my head. If Joe did know Belken, he was a pretty good actor.

George and Max's voices were growing closer to where we were sitting, so I lowered my voice. "Surely the police gave you the name."

He shook his head, as if thinking. "No, they didn't. Oh, they did mention someone when I was in the hospital. I was on a lot of pain meds."

I nodded. "Those'll fry your brain. Do you think this Barry Belken and Talbot Peters could be the same guy?"

George had heard me say Talbot's name and peered over the service counter at Joe and me. "Yeah, Joe, I'm sorry about that. I was going to tell you. He didn't steal a dime."

Not this time.

"You don't owe me any apologies, George."

Max called for George to help him find a dust pan, so George walked toward the back.

Joe met my eyes and it was clear he would not answer. "You look tired. I'm sorry if I upset you." *Not really.*

"Not your fault." He pointed at his sling. "Makes me want

to get better faster. So you, uh, never saw the Talbot guy again?"

"No." I glanced toward the back of the shop. "You really think Max can help?"

Joe lowered his voice. "Nah, but he'll be good company when I'm here alone. Once people know he got hurt in Iraq they don't mind his talking so much."

"You're a good sport," I said.

His expression was unreadable. "I'm learning."

As I left Java Jolt my mobile phone chirped. When the caller ID indicated who it was, I groaned. "Hello."

Morehouse sounded really, really angry. "What the hell did you want at the station this morning?"

"That front desk officer sounds like a bit of a tattle tale."

"Dammit," he began.

"I had an idea about that car accident in front of Markle's store being related to Joe's shooting."

"Yeah, I heard that's what you asked. I'm tired, really tired of telling you to butt out."

"Was it a man or woman who called to tell you Joe wasn't in Java Jolt that morning?"

I held the phone away from my ear. All I could make out were words like "could have been killed," and "dangerous business."

In a stroke of probably not very good sense, I adopted Morehouse's habit and hung up without saying good-bye.

He called back. "Does it ever occur to you that Ocean Alley police do more than sit around with our thumbs in our ears?"

"On a daily basis," I replied, quickly. "Sometimes I just have ideas…"

"Do not come down here again unless you are reporting a crime or providing information." He hung up.

I DID STOP by Java Jolt Friday morning. Joe's hand was swollen after being there for a few hours on Thursday, and Aunt Madge ordered him to stay at the Cozy Corner to keep it elevated. I should probably teach Joe how to get around her edicts, but since he won't be there long there's no need. *And since he's probably lying to me about a bunch of stuff, I'm not sure I care if his fingers are swollen.*

George moved the heavy thermoses of coffee around and I poured individual cups as needed until the morning rush was over. Then I left for the courthouse to finish finding houses to compare to the ones I was appraising. All three were typical Ocean Alley bungalows, with frame exteriors that had been replaced by vinyl siding.

Two had beautiful interiors, but the third had been primarily a summer cottage. From Lester's comments on some notes he sent to Harry and me, the owner of the third one had unrealistic expectations as to what the house was worth. A buyer from Connecticut had been willing to match the asking price, but I didn't think even the most creative appraisal language was going to let me uphold the value to support the mortgage the buyer wanted. When even Lester is aware of this, it's clear that the negotiated sales price on a real estate contract is really too high.

I reviewed my notes, decided the third house would take serious consultation with Harry, and stopped at Burger King for a salad before heading back to Java Jolt. For someone who had decided to do less, I was paying too much attention to it. I told myself I wanted to see how Max was doing.

I found a parking spot just off the boardwalk and half-jogged from the top of the steps to Java Jolt. I had barely jogged or power walked for two weeks. "Slug," I said, aloud.

At the entrance to Java Jolt I stopped. The closed sign was facing me. *Why is that?* I pushed the door and it opened. "George? Max?"

I heard the back door slam. "Max? George?"

"It's me, Jolie. Me." Max came down the back hallway and stopped at the service side of the counter. He looked...odd. Sort of ill at ease, except that's hard to tell with Max.

"Where is George? Did he take the trash out?"

"The bank. George is at the bank."

I felt myself flush. "He left you alone?"

"I said okay, okay."

The door to the boardwalk opened again and George stood there, looking perplexed. "Why are we closed?"

"Gee, I don't know. Maybe because Max was here *alone*?" I glared at George.

"We didn't close....I mean, it was only for a minute." George flipped the sign back to open.

I looked at Max again. Something was wrong. "What happened, Max?"

He frowned, looking confused. "I don't think that man liked me."

George and I said, together, "What man?"

"The one in the sweatshirt, and sunglasses. Sunglasses."

"Is that who went out the back door?" I asked.

Max nodded. "He wanted Joe. I said no Joe, no Joe. He didn't believe me. Do you want to go to Newhart's with me, Jolie? To see Arnie? Arnie?"

"Sure Max." I wanted to throw a sugar canister at George, but resisted. "How about a milk shake?"

Max took off the Java Jolt apron he wore. "You like milk shakes, Jolie. I like donuts, donuts."

MAX AND I WENT from Newhart's to my house and waited for Scoobie to come home from work. Max had not been anxious to talk about the man who was looking for Joe, and I didn't push him. But I didn't want to leave him alone at his house.

Max was on the floor in the bedroom, talking to Pebbles. I dialed George's cell. "What were you thinking?" It's hard to convey anger when you have to keep your voice down.

"I honest to God thought leaving him for ten minutes was fine. Reverend Jamison's secretary and her sister were in there when I went to the bank. No one else."

"Except Max, alone!"

George tried to mollify me. "Okay, okay. You're right. I shouldn't have left him alone. Did he, uh, say who it was?"

"He didn't know him. Something about the guy made him nervous. I brought Max to our house to talk to Scoobie."

George called to someone, apparently a customer. "Be right with you."

"Go," I said. "Scoobie can talk to you later." I certainly didn't want to.

"THE THING IS, Jolie, I don't know what we'd say if we called the police. And talking to them would make Max nervous." Scoobie glanced toward the bedroom as he spoke. Max was again lying on the bedroom floor looking at Pebbles.

"*You* don't want to call the police?" I teased.

"What would we tell the cops? Someone looked for Joe? The person didn't stick around, and Max can't or won't describe him."

"I guess. But still…"

"Max didn't like the guy, but right now all he's concerned about is eating some of the brownies you're making and getting home to watch the movie he rented today."

"What movie?" I asked, not wanting to debate whether to tell the police.

"You care?"

"No. I don't know why I asked."

"*Sound of Music*. He likes the scene where the kids hang from the trees."

"How do you know that?" I asked.

"I listen."

Max walked into the living room. "I listen. I forget, too."

I laughed. I had to. "Me, too."

"You want help cutting the brownies? Should we save some for Joe? For Joe?"

I stood from where I'd been sitting on the couch. "I bet he'd like some."

"Did you put in all the ingredients this time?" Scoobie asked.

"I helped, helped," Max said.

"He read me the recipe." I shook a finger at Scoobie. "Max likes my cooking."

"Except your mashed potatoes," Max said.

Scoobie hid his laugh with a cough. "George and I are going to an AA meeting tonight, Max. You want to come?"

I was surprised. "Max, I uh, didn't know you went to

those. I go sometimes, too." When Max looked at me, I said, "I go to the All-Anon meetings. You know, for families."

"You don't go much," Max informed me. "Me either, me either. I went with Josh."

"Ah, Josh. He was your good friend."

Max nodded, subdued. "I miss him. He'll be back some day. Some day."

I looked at Scoobie and he shrugged. "Want to come, Max?"

"No. Brownies, then movie, then bed."

"Um, here?" I asked.

Max's look implied patience. "I'm going home to watch my movie."

The timer dinged and Max walked the short distance to the kitchen. I looked at Scoobie. "George is supposed to be at the party tomorrow. I don't know if Max and Joe should be alone at Java Jolt."

"Max says he's coming to the Halloween party, as long as it's not too noisy." Scoobie shrugged. "Java Jolt's crowded on Saturdays. George'll go by before and after. It's the off-season and Joe knows the patrons. Somebody'll lift thermoses or whatever he needs."

"What if that guy comes back?"

"You remember the bit about admitting you have no control?"

"I remember. I just don't like it."

After Scoobie and Max left, I sat on the couch, Jazz in my lap, and stared ahead, thinking. It puzzled me that the police were not questioning Joe more. He'd been shot, so they might go easier on him. But still, Barry Belken had been at Java Jolt, whether Joe knew him or not. Yet Joe had looked genuinely surprised when I mentioned Belken's name, so maybe the police had not asked Joe about him again. Was Joe lying to me?

Maybe Talbot Peters was a cleaned-up, somewhat heavier version of Barry Belken, but I couldn't be at all sure. I wished I had access to tapes from the security cameras at the courthouse. It would be good to have a photo of the so-called Talbot Peters talking to me the day he introduced himself.

Talbot's face was fuller, and of course he had no facial hair. His hair was short, and he didn't act sullen, which was the Belken expression. But there was the different eye color. *Contact lenses come in colors.*

I sighed. No one would show the courthouse camera feeds to me, so no point thinking about it.

My stomach roiled. I had not told Scoobie I wondered whether Belken and Peters could be the same person. No point thinking about that. I wasn't sure what I wanted to do about telling Scoobie. Besides not having to deal with it.

CHAPTER FIFTEEN

IT FELT ODD TO be at a Harvest for All fundraiser and not be running around like a pebble peeper bird on the beach. Dr. Welby had been true to his word about making nearly all the arrangements. All I had done was place radio ads and make sure we had volunteers to collect the donated canned goods. And Megan had helped with that.

Most chairs in the country club's large dining room had been removed, though there were small tables and a few chairs around two sides. Hanging from the ceiling was a large, burro-shaped piñata, which was filled with candy and small toys. I was apprehensive about kids swinging bats or sticks at the burro to open the flood of goodies. Heck, not kids, a couple of the adults.

Scoobie called from the other side of the room. "Yo, Jolie. Time to get your costume on."

I glanced toward him and started to laugh. He left the house after I did, and had been secretive about his costume.

Scoobie was a book. It looked as if he had taken a box that could have held a washing machine and cut it so that it was shorter and not as wide. It had been painted beige and someone had drawn an open book on the front. Only his face showed amid his head gear. As I walked toward him it became clear his head was a light bulb.

"It's really good." I couldn't lean across his box, so I kissed my fingers and touched his cheek.

Scoobie grinned. "I've heard it's hard to read me sometimes, so I thought this might help."

I groaned, and a man's voice behind me said, "Is it something I would want to read?"

Reverend Jamison stood next to me, smiling as he read. The left-hand page had a list of Scoobie's favorite books and the right had one of his poems.

in the fuzzy land
between asleep and awake
homesick dreams
fly with angels
where they were born
they'll never die
so she said...
like indian summer
was almost asleep
serendipity drummer
loud colors creep
memory awaken
future too late
dream not forsaken
well worth the wait

"How come it doesn't have a name?" I asked.

"Because I haven't decided on one, yet," Scoobie said.

Reverend Jamison pointed to the poem. "I like fly with angels."

"You would." Lance Wilson was dressed as a cowboy, complete with chaps and a red bandana around his neck.

"Where did you get that?" I asked, laughing.

"The Internet. Best sixty dollars I ever spent."

Renée's voice came from behind me and I whirled to face her. "Sixty dollars is cheap for an adult costume these days."

"You came! Wow!" Renée had on a very light green, mid-calf length outfit made of tulle, with a petticoat to make it puffy. She had sewn a number of stars on the dress. From their shape it looked as if her daughters had cut them out. Renée's wand had a large star on one end.

I started to hug my sister, but her daughter Michelle pointed a wand at me and frowned. "You can't hug the queen of the fairies." She and her sister Julia were their mother in miniature, except one wore pink and the other light blue. Julia, who is twenty months older than Michelle's six years, also raised her wand.

Renée laughed as she spoke. "Sisters can hug."

"Only when they wear their costumes," Michelle said. Ever since she started first grade she's very sure of her opinions.

"Where is your costume, Aunt Jolie?" Julia asked.

Renée nodded at Reverend Jamison and waved at Scoobie, who said, "Glad you brought your minions."

I looked at my nieces, who were gazing at me intently. "I'm going to get changed now. When I come back you can guess who I am."

"Does it involve a witch's hat?" George asked, from behind me.

"I'm not talking to you," I said, and faced him.

"Ha! You just did." He walked toward Tiffany, who was scribbling in her reporter's notebook.

Renée looked around the room and then at me. "Nice digs. We came early to see if you needed help."

Scoobie and Reverend Jamison, who had handed each of the girls a lollipop, walked off to examine the two large tables that were to hold canned food donations.

"Dr. Welby and Sylvia Parrett thought if we went upscale we'd get some new donors."

Renée lowered her voice. "Can you make money if you spend this much for a room and food?"

"We aren't spending anything. The club donated use of the room, and probably discounted the food. Dr. Welby got a bunch of his doctor pals to donate money for food. Some of them even wrote checks on top of that."

"Wow," she said, and then made a shooing gesture. "Go get changed."

I walked with a light step toward the women's restroom. When I lived in Lakewood I saw my nieces at least two or three times a month. Though I'd seen them a number of times the last three years, I was no longer a regular part of their lives.

Visits to Ocean Alley required planning, and meant Julia and Michelle would be away from friends and regular activities. Friends are a high priority at their ages. I understood this completely.

It was my fault that we didn't establish any kind of schedule for aunt-and-niece get togethers. The first few months after my marriage dissolved I was barely fit to take care of myself.

But that was then and this is now. I saw today as the first of many afternoons together. Happy days.

WHEN I GOT BACK TO the party room there were about fifty people milling around. I stood in the doorway for a moment and watched my younger niece throw a beanbag into a clown's open mouth. It was our only continuing game.

Aunt Madge and Harry had organized a pin-the-tail-on-the-donkey game that would start in about half an hour. They had brought several poster-boards of painted donkeys, thinking there would be a lot of players. They had also brought two bulletin boards, about one meter square each, to hang the donkeys on. The poster board and bulletin boards were leaning against one wall for now.

Monica, minus her usual role running the bake sale table, was painting fake tattoos on children. *I had no idea she could paint.*

A boy walked by me rubbing something off his face. It looked like a bent star. *I guess she can't paint.*

Food tables had some sugar cookies in Halloween shapes, but most of the food was not sweet, unless you counted the large tray of fruit. There were pretzels, cheese and crackers, and a vegetable plate with dip. I looked at a pile of small plastic storage containers because I couldn't tell what they were. They were only two inches or so in diameter. Closer inspection showed they held Cheerios.

Sylvia appeared to be guarding those, and I complimented her on having something for really little kids.

A donation jar sat near the entrance, but we did not charge an admission fee. What mattered was that two tables were already loaded with canned and boxed food and there were envelopes in the jar. Megan's daughter Alicia, dressed as a flamingo dancer, was overseeing a couple of her high school classmates as the boys packed boxes. They would be the only older kids here, as our publicity said the party was geared to ages twelve and younger.

Two clowns walked in, each carrying a duffel bag. I had forgotten that we were having clown jugglers to keep kids entertained.

I walked up to the country club employee who was in charge. At least he seemed to be, since he directed the servers who kept tables supplied with food. "Is there, um, something I can do?"

He regarded my tall witch's cap and the cotton bathrobe I had dyed blue and painted with stars. "Who are you?"

"I'm Jolie Gen..."

He grinned. "I meant your costume."

I smiled back. "Hermione from the Harry Potter stories."

"Minus the bushy hair," he said. "Nope, don't need any help. Dr. Welby said you were supposed to relax."

I kind of smirked. "How about Scoobie?"

He frowned slightly. "I'm not sure what Dr. Welby meant when he said he hoped Scoobie didn't pull anything."

We both turned toward the source of a lot of laughter and shrieks from children. Someone in a Darth Vadar costume had arrived. He had rigged up something near his mouth so his breath sounded like the raspy hiss of the movie character.

The country club employee turned to inspect food on the tables, and I stared at the costume. *That must have cost a fortune.*

Harry walked up to me. "Who's Darth Vader?"

"No idea."

"Do you know if we're having a best costume contest?" Harry asked.

"Hmm. We didn't talk about it at our planning meetings." My eyes wandered to Dr. Welby and Aretha, who were passing out candy they held in plastic pumpkins. "We'd just create losers."

"Good point. I'm the one in charge of keeping track of the numbered donkey darts. I wish we had bought those magnet darts and their boards, but they were awfully expensive." He saw Aunt Madge, who had just come in wearing her Wonder Woman outfit, and walked toward her. I waved to her, and she raised a fist in my direction.

"You did wear a witch's hat."

I turned to face George. "I'm a good witch, and I'm still not talking to you."

"C'mon, Jolie. Max is fine. He thinks it was all a big adventure."

"He could have been kidnapped and he'd be dead by now."

"You need a meeting," George said, and walked away.

I need a meeting? Oh, forgiveness. He was right. My fear for Max had taken over my temperament. I started to follow George, but Renée called my name and I turned to see her on the opposite side of the room. *Later, George.*

She met me halfway and handed me a tiny cup of candy corn. "Aunt Madge says she and Harry need more help for the donkey tail game than they thought they would. Lots more kids. Can you keep an eye on the girls?"

"Of course. I'll round them up when I hear Aunt Madge or Harry announce the game is starting."

Renée went back toward Aunt Madge and I watched Darth Vadar let kids get enveloped in his cape. He stood at the edge of room, and opened the cape with his light saber. Men and boys seemed most enamored with Darth.

Scoobie caught my eye and gestured with his head that I should come to him. I had no idea how he planned to use his arms today.

"Yo, Jolie," he said. "I have a bunch of bookmarks in a sort of pocket on the spine of my book. Can you make a little sign that says take one?"

I peered at his back. The images on the back were the book's front and back covers. The spine bore the words "Welcome to Reading." I laughed. Two huge photos were glued to each cover. On the front cover were Aunt Madge's two retrievers. Mr. Rogers bore a scarf that said 'Read' and Miss Piggy had one that said 'Me." Hers was crooked, likely because she had been trying to paw it off. The back cover had Jazz and Pebbles. Jazz was sitting on a book, and Pebbles was smelling it.

"You worked on this for a long time," I said. "I would have helped you."

"I helped, Jolie, I helped."

I turned to see Max, who was dressed as a baker, complete with a puffy top hat. His white coat was probably a lab coat from the hospital. "You look good."

He beamed. "I like sweets. Sweets. Aunt Madge made my hat."

"She did," Scoobie said. Max walked away, and in a lowered voice, Scoobie added, "We did it at his house. George and I thought it would be good if people were seen going in and out."

I felt kind of left out, but George and Scoobie had been doing things together for about fifteen years. No reason they had to include me all the time. *Especially when you aren't talking to George.*

Using a marker and small piece of paper commandeered from the registration table, I made a sign that said, "Free, take one," and walked back to Scoobie to tape it to the spine of his book. The bookmarks had a pumpkin and the words "Harvest for All," complete with the food pantry address and hours of operation.

"Ladies and gents!" Dr. Welby certainly didn't need the microphone he held. "Madge and Harry and helpers are getting ready to start the Pin-the-Tail-on-the-Donkey game. You can see we have two donkeys, so we'll have two lines. While you wait you can watch our juggling clowns."

He continued with instructions for where the lines would form. About fifty enthusiastic witches, ghosts, spiders, and various action-figure characters started to get in the two lines. Roughly fifty adults, parents I assumed, snapped pictures of the kids from every angle.

Aretha and Daphne walked over to me. "We've been designated, with Megan, to be blindfolded and swing at the piñata." Daphne smiled as she said this. She had accented her cafe-au-lait skin color with peel-off tatoos in the shape of leaves in fall colors.

"Lucky you." I gestured they should walk with me. "I have to keep an eye on my nieces. No guys?"

"Apparently," Aretha grinned, "Dr. Welby and others thought the guys who help most often would be a tad boisterous."

"No kidding," I said, dryly. We had gotten closer to the donkey game. Renée's older daughter had apparently insisted on helping Aunt Madge. While Julia looked busy, Michelle stood to one side looking forlorn.

I waved to her to come to me, and she walked slowly.

Daphne whispered. "I think you're supposed to feel sorry for her."

"Yep." Then I raised my voice and spoke to Michelle. "Come on, I haven't eaten anything yet. Have you?"

"The cookies are great," Aretha said, and held her hand out to Michelle, who immediately went into shy mode and took my hand.

Aretha laughed as the two walked away. Daphne said, "Make sure you try the cookies."

"Yes ma'am," Michelle said.

We filled our plates without talking too much, and moved to an unoccupied table at the edge of the room. We stopped eating a number of times to see why people were shrieking at the donkey game. Usually it meant someone was getting close to the donkey's back side.

Someone dressed as a striped cat handed Michelle a popcorn ball, and she took it, uncertain what to do. The cat, who had on a full mask, squeaked, "Good popcorn," and walked toward the piñata. Michelle looked up at me, with a questioning expression.

"It's popcorn with syrup or caramel to make the kernels stick together."

"It's wrapped, but it's sticky," she said, and handed the ball to me.

I placed the popcorn ball on the table. "You going to try to pin the tail? It looks like everyone gets a piece of candy or a prize."

She shook her head. "I don't want the blindfold."

"Ah. I don't blame you." We turned our attention to the piñata, and I explained that she would have to move fast to pick up the goodies as they fell.

Lance came to sit with us, and we watched the donkey game wind down. Dr. Welby and George stood under the piñata. George held three sticks, which looked like mop handles, that Aretha, Megan, and Daphne would use to swing, blindfolded, at the paper maché donkey.

Scoobie walked over and stood next to us. "Guess you can't sit down," Lance said to him.

"Nope, but I'm on my feet all day, so I'm used to it." He studied the piñata. "What do you suppose it says that we have jackasses in today's biggest games?"

"If you mean George..." I began.

"What's a jackass?" Michelle asked.

Scoobie winced. "A sort of impolite term for donkey."

Lance laughed. "Now you did it."

Michelle's expression was very serious. "If you don't say it again I won't tell my mom."

Scoobie matched her demeanor. Or as much as one can when dressed like a book. "I will not say that again."

"Okay." She slid off her seat. "I need to get ready for the treats."

I stood and looked at Scoobie, smiling. "You got off easy." I nodded toward Michelle. "My job to keep track of her for a bit longer."

As the donkey game ended, most of the guests had migrated to the area not far from the largest of the several doors that led into the room, where the piñata hung from the ceiling. There would have been more room to circle under it in the center of the room, but a huge chandelier hung there. The last thing we needed was to have someone swat it.

Dr. Welby stood on a sturdy wooden box near the piñata and called to me. "Jolie, your turn."

We had agreed that I would thank the attendees at some point, but I had left it to him to decide when. It's always tough to predict how events will flow. I looked at Michelle. "Stay with Scoobie, kiddo."

Michelle nodded, and kept staring at the piñata.

I let Dr. Welby help me onto the box and glanced at the roughly one-hundred-fifty attendees. All but a few of the parents were in costume, too. "Gosh, thank you so much for coming. I bet a lot of you brought cans of food to help neighbors."

A loud boy's voice came from the center of the crowd. "Macaroni and cheese comes in *boxes.*"

I laughed. "It does. I love mac and cheese."

Darth Vadar raised his light saber as if toasting me.

"I won't talk long, because I know you want to see what's inside the piñata." I gestured toward it. "Please remember Harvest for All when you do volunteer projects at school or church. You might think you can't do much, but it's when we all work together that we help the most people. If you want to see what we do, feel free to drop by the pantry at First Presbyterian. The hours are on the bookmarks that Scoobie is distributing." I pointed to him and he turned so that the back book covers and spine faced the crowd. "And thanks again."

George stood next to the soap box and held a hand to help me down. He grinned. "Try not to fall on your tush."

Monica was just behind him. "Oh dear, don't."

I smiled at her. "No worries."

George followed me to where Scoobie and Michelle were standing, not far from Darth Vadar, who was again enveloping little boys in his cloak for a few moments each.

"We're talking again," I said.

George grinned. "My Halloween treat."

"Don't let it go to your head," Scoobie said.

I ignored them both and looked at my niece. "Are you excited, Michelle?"

She crooked her finger at me and I bent down to her. "Will it hurt the donkey to get hit?"

"No. It's a pretend donkey. He's mostly made of paper."

Michelle looked relieved. Scoobie met my eyes and raised his eyebrows up and down. Neither one of us wanted her to see us laugh at her question.

Dr. Welby had finished introducing Daphne, Megan, and Aretha, and explained that they would not all swing at the same time because he didn't want them to hit each other.

"Aw, shucks," a boy's voice said, and people laughed.

After five minutes, I could tell the piñata bashing was going to take a while. We should have had a back-up plan. Maybe swinging without the blindfolds after ten minutes.

Another five minutes went by and I realized I hadn't seen Michelle in a couple of minutes. Renée was done with the pin-the-tail-on-the-donkey game, but I had not formally relinquished my duty for eyes on Michelle.

Scoobie was on the other side of the room, talking to Renée. I scanned the crowd and still didn't see Michelle. "George."

He walked to me. "Oh, good, you're still talking…"

"Do you see Michelle?"

As he began to look into the crowd of squealing children, someone in a pig costume, complete with pig's head, waved a small envelope in front of me. When I took it, the pig squeaked, "Oink," and hurried away.

I was about to stick the envelope in my pocket when George said, very stridently, "Open it."

"I need to keep looking for…"

"Open it," he repeated.

I felt cold all over and my stomach did a flip flop as I tore open the envelope.

The brief note was written in block letters with a black pen. All it said was, "We've got the little girl. Go to Java Jolt--alone. After he gives you the money, someone will call to tell you where to trade for her. No police."

CHAPTER SIXTEEN

I USUALLY THINK FAST, but not now. George said, "Walk toward your car. I'll tell Renée you took Michelle to the ladies room. Be right behind you."

For some reason I obeyed. As I crossed the room my eyes took in the spot where Darth Vadar had been standing. He was gone.

Does that mean anything? Could he have grabbed her under his cloak? Surely Michelle would have screamed. And where did that pig come from? I didn't think I'd seen him (or her?) until he walked up.

Everyone was in the country club dining room watching the piñata get whacked so no one passed me in the hall. I ran into the parking lot, thankful that while my purse was still hidden under the food donation table, I had a car key in my pocket from when I'd unloaded the clipboards and sign-in sheets.

I got to my Toyota and dropped the key as I tried to open the door. "Damn!" I grabbed it off the asphalt, inserted it to unlock the door, and pulled the door open so hard I almost knocked myself over.

My tires screeched as I pulled out of the parking lot. In my rear view mirror I saw George come out of the building and wave, but I wasn't going to stop.

As I got to the end of the driveway I slowed to turn onto Sandy Shore Drive. I talked to myself. "Calm down. Calm down. Does Joe have the money they want? Will he be at Java Jolt?" The country club was about half a mile from Java Jolt. I wanted to pound on my horn as I got closer to the boardwalk, but kept my cool.

My car window was partially down and I smelled the ocean as I pulled into a parking spot just off the boardwalk. *How can such a peaceful place have child kidnappers?* As I rushed out of the car my bathrobe caught in the closing door and I shrugged it off.

Why can't there be a lot of people on the boardwalk now? Or maybe I didn't want people there. Maybe I shouldn't call attention to myself.

The flight of steps up to the boardwalk never seemed so tall. I jogged to the door of Java Jolt, and stopped at the "Closed for the afternoon" sign. "What the...?" The door was locked.

I pounded on the door. No response. I had never felt so helpless.

I turned and ran toward the boardwalk stairs. Seven steps to the street below the boardwalk, just around the corner to Java Jolt's back door.

"Jolie!" I heard someone yell hello, but I didn't stop.

I need to get to the alley behind the boardwalk shops. I can break the glass in the back door. I can break the glass in the back door.

I ran up the few steps that took me to the stoop at the back of the coffee shop. I shook the handle. It was locked, so I pounded on the glass that covered a good portion of the door.

When no one responded, I peered in. Joe Regan was sitting on the floor leaning against the wall not far from the door. My pounding roused him, and he blinked his eyes to focus on me. I couldn't hear him, but I could read his lips. "Break it."

Like I carry a crow bar.

Frantic, I swirled and looked up and down the alley. Garbage bags flowed out of the dumpster, and one was hanging down, partially opened. A wine bottle protruded. I ran to the dumpster and grabbed the dark green bottle that looked as if it had a thick bottom.

The glass in the door was single pane. It should be breakable. I ran up the back steps again, covered my eyes with one hand, and swung as hard as I could. "Nuts!" The glass had a bunch of cracks spreading outward from where the wine bottle had hit. I raised it again, eyes covered, and aimed for the same spot.

This time the smash was accompanied by a few tinkles of glass. It was enough for me to stick a couple fingers through the hole and jiggle the glass with my thumb and forefinger. It took about ten seconds, but more glass fell into the store and I reached in and unlocked the door handle.

A closer look showed Joe's left eye was blackened and almost shut.

"Where, Joe? The note said you had money I can trade for my six-year old niece."

"You'll have to get it out." He raised his cast a few inches in explanation and pointed to the wall, just above my head.

"Where is it? Hurry up!"

"Behind the thermostat." He took a Phillips screwdriver from his sling and I bent over to take it from him.

I stared at the screwdriver for a second and then looked at Joe. "Is the electricity off?"

He shook his head. "It's fake. When you undo the screws you'll see."

I had started on them before he finished talking. My mobile phone chirped and I ignored it. Then I thought it might be the kidnappers, so I pulled it out and put it on my shoulder, balancing it with my tilted head.

It was Scoobie. "Where are you?" The screech of tires on pavement told me he was in a car.

"I'm at Java Jolt. Joe's showing me where the money is hidden."

"I called Morehouse. He's in civvies, not far from you. He's getting some others to..." Scoobie was shouting, so Joe heard his words.

Joe groaned and raised his voice so Scoobie could hear. "They can't see police."

George's voice came through. He must have been driving, since it was fainter than Scoobie's. "You know how to contact them when you have the money?"

The fake thermostat fell to the floor. There were no wires behind it, and I peered in. It was as dark as Darth Vadar's costume.

"Reach your hand in," Joe said. "It's not far back."

Joe's had it all along. I believed him!

I groped and came up with two plastic bags that seemed to be full of paper. Heavy paper. I pulled them toward me. "Is this it?"

"Yeah. Wiggle it a bit and you can pull it out."

How did I not even hear Michelle scream? What have they done with her?

Scoobie yelled through the phone. "Don't leave there. Stay in Java Jolt."

Phone balancing was getting more tenuous, and the phone fell to the floor. The back of the phone came off and the battery skidded across the floor.

I finished pulling the money out and looked at Joe. "Now what? Where do I take it?"

Before he could answer his mobile phone rang, to the tune of *When Irish Eyes are Smiling*.

It was also stored in his sling, and he pulled it out, pushed a button, and said one word. "Where?" He listened for a second, and said, "She can't… Dammit!"

Apparently the caller had hung up.

"Where are we going?" I asked.

Joe's face was pinched, probably in pain. "They said only you. To the kids' carousel at the end of the boardwalk." He handed me his phone. "They'll call you there."

I stared at him, then snatched the phone from his hand and stuffed it in my pocket. As I turned one plastic bag broke and about ten bundles of fifty and hundred dollar bills fell to the floor. I grabbed an oversized plastic tub of coffee on a shelf near the back door, turned it over to empty the coffee on the floor, and began stuffing bundles of bills into it.

Joe had risen and was leaning against the wall. "Be careful. Don't go with them."

I stumbled as I stood and made my way to the front door, which led to the boardwalk. As I opened it, I thought I heard Joe say, "I'm sorry."

Ground to a Halt

THE CAROUSEL WAS less than one-quarter of a mile down the boardwalk from Java Jolt. I turned in that direction and found myself walking against the wind. The tall witch's hat, which I'd forgotten was on my head, started to blow off. I grabbed for it and held it on with the hand not holding the coffee tub. The container was plastic and about half the size of a bathroom trash can. Still, it was awkward to carry. *Who knew dollar bills were so heavy?*

In the off-season, the closed children's ride area at the end of the Ocean Alley boardwalk is more like a deserted factory than a play area. It's roofed, but there is a wall on only one side. The four rides are not large, and the bumper cars were not even on their floor. The small carousel was in the middle of the space.

I stopped at the edge of the area and walked slowly toward the carousel. Lighting was dim, and it took a few moments for me to see the piece of paper taped to the tallest horse. I grabbed it and read. "Walk down the steps nearest to here and look for the pig."

The pig? From the party? I dropped the note and ran. The boardwalk was about ten steps above the street at this point, and I raced down the wooden staircase. As I got to the bottom, the pig stepped from the alley that runs behind the boardwalk buildings and gestured that I should come to him.

With only a few seconds' hesitation, I complied. As I got closer, I realized the pig was not much taller than I was. *Could it be a woman?* I tilted the coffee tub so the pig could see the money. He (or she?) gestured to someone in the alley. Then, as he lunged at me to grab the money, he spoke in a falsetto. "You tell the police anything about us, and Joe's dead." He turned to run toward B Street.

"Where's Michelle?!"

Michelle walked out of the alley, saw me, raised her arms, and burst into tears.

I knelt and enveloped her. "It's okay, baby. You're safe."

Her sobs came in gulps. "I'm sorry, Aunt Jolie. Mommy will be so mad!" Her crying was continual now, no room for words.

"Nobody's mad at you sweetie. You're such a good girl." I hugged her tighter.

I heard sirens in the distance and voices above me, on the boardwalk. "Where the hell is she?" That sounded like Morehouse.

"Wait, there's a note!" That was definitely Dana.

I stood, picking up Michelle and turning toward the boardwalk so I could yell. "We're here!"

Morehouse came down the steps at top speed. Dana was right behind him. He barely slowed as he got closer. "You see 'em?"

"Ran toward B Street. Dressed like a pig." I said the last few words to his back, and saw Morehouse pull a gun from a shoulder holster as he ran.

"Call your sister," Dana gasped, as she ran after him. She pulled a radio from her belt. "All units, B and…" her words trailed off.

The activity seemed to calm Michelle, and her sobs grew quieter. "Call mommy," she whispered.

I shifted her to my left hip and reached in my pocket for a phone. But it was Joe's, not mine. Mine was on the floor at

Java Jolt. That meant no speed dial for Renée. "What's mommy's mobile number, sweetie?"

Michelle concurrently sniffed and wiped her nose on my shoulder, reciting the ten-digit number as she did so.

"You're such a smart girl," I murmured.

On the boardwalk above, more running feet were coming toward us. Renée answered the phone. "Who are you? Where is my…"

"Renée. I have her. She's okay."

CHAPTER SEVENTEEN

THE PIG WAS LONG gone in the minute before the police got to us. Or they could have walked right by him at some point. I heard Dana's radio when someone said the pig head was in a dumpster a block away from the carousel. I didn't really care.

Michelle was in my crowded living room on her mom's lap and Julia leaned against Scoobie, who was seated on one of the dinette chairs. All I wanted to do was find Joe Regan and maim him. Badly. The pig's words rattled around my brain. "You tell the police anything about us, and Joe's dead."

I wanted Joe in prison for a long time. Dead? Maybe not so much. But the pig's threat wasn't going to stop me from telling the police what I knew. Most of it, anyway.

The storm door opened and shut firmly. My brother-in-law walked in and scooped Julia from Scoobie. Michelle jumped off Renée's lap and grabbed her father by the legs.

Renée stood and she joined Andrew and the girls in a family hug. After a few moments, Andrew looked over the top of them, to me. "What the hell happened, Jolie?"

"Someone took Michelle, to encourage Joe to give them some money…" I began.

"Who is Joe?" Andrew asked, releasing Renée and the girls.

The front door opened so hard it hit the wall and Morehouse walked in, with Dana and George behind him. We all stopped talking. Finally, Scoobie asked, "You found Max?"

Andrew, a frown deepening, said, "I want to know…"

Morehouse raised a palm, kind of like a school patrol at the bus stop. His expression was grim. "Everybody have a seat. I'll tell you all at the same time." He looked at Scoobie. "Yes. He was still at the club. He's going to hang at Markle's grocery place for a couple of hours."

I hadn't given Max a thought for the first few minutes after we found Michelle. If the criminal crew was doing clean-up, Max could be on their list to trash.

Aunt Madge and Harry walked in from the kitchen where she had been making tea. As we seated ourselves around the living room, she looked at Morehouse. "Can you get the cars to stop those red and blue flashing lights?"

"Sure." He walked into the hallway, opened the storm door and yelled something to the officers attached to the two police cars that sat in front of my house. In a few seconds the lights were off.

I didn't see the point of the cars. Whoever had the money wanted to get away from us, not drop by for a visit.

Dana leaned against the door jamb that separates the combined living/dining room from the hall, her gaze roaming among us.

"Okay." Morehouse flipped open his notebook and thumbed a few pages. "Michelle here," he smiled at her, "was taken from the country club main dining room at about three-thirty. We aren't sure by who yet."

He glanced at her again, now secure on her father's lap. When he had tried to ask her questions a few minutes ago she had simply buried her face in Renée's shoulder, and he didn't push her.

"Darth Vadar," Michelle said, softly. "He's bad. But the pig was nice to me."

"Yes, Darth Vadar is very bad," Morehouse said. But as he smiled at her he nodded to Dana, who walked outside. Then Morehouse looked at me. "Who was in those costumes?"

"I wish I knew." I looked at Scoobie.

"I don't' think the Darth Vadar guy said a word all afternoon, and I never saw the pig." Scoobie looked at George.

George frowned for a second. "Didn't hear Darth Vadar talk, but maybe Tiffany tried to interview him." He pulled out his mobile phone and walked into the kitchen.

"Why? Why Michelle?" Andrew asked.

I'd told Renée a bit about Joe insisting he didn't have the cash from a Kansas robbery years ago, but that was all we'd had time to discuss. Our focus had been on her girls.

"Not likely they knew your daughter," Morehouse said, looking at Andrew and Renée.

I had not introduced Andrew. Morehouse had guessed the obvious.

Morehouse continued. "They may even have wanted to target Jolie, though she'd be harder to handle. Maybe thought they could get her away from the Halloween party, or something."

"Me?" I squeaked.

Morehouse shrugged. "Maybe. Did a lot of people know Renée and the girls would be here today?"

"No," Renée said, "I wasn't totally sure until this morning, and we don't usually come to the fundraisers."

"How?" Scoobie asked, his voice strained. "How did they link Jolie to Joe and the money he had?"

Andrew started to ask who Joe Regan was, but Morehouse raised a finger at him and said, "He owns the coffee shop. Could be because she visited him in the hospital and's been talking to him in Java Jolt." He scowled at me. "Probably probing a lot about the shooting."

Andrew is a big man, almost six-two, weighing maybe two-hundred forty pounds, which he carries well. I'd never thought of him as intimidating before. He didn't exactly shout, but almost. "Shooting!"

Michelle looked as if she might cry again, and Andrew stroked her hair.

I looked at him directly. "I was on the street when Joe was shot around the corner. Then he came toward me. It was nothing to do with me." I looked at Morehouse. "But I can't get it out of my head."

Renée said, "Madge called me at the time. I didn't think much about it."

She and Andrew looked at each other for a moment, and I figured they'd talk more later.

Morehouse continued. "Joe was obviously involved in that robbery in Kansas, though he kept that from all of us." He looked at me. "My guess is his partners, or whoever they are, think you're his girlfriend and expected you to know where he hid the money. Or figured he'd give them the money to save you."

"He was pretty convincing about not being involved," Dana said. "I believed him."

"Me, too," Scoobie said.

I looked at Morehouse. "What happened to Joe? I mean, after." I didn't need to say after what.

"Joe's gone," Morehouse said. "Did he say anything to you about where he was going?"

"We didn't exactly talk. You saw where he kept his money, right?"

Morehouse nodded. "Pretty good hiding place."

George was back in the room. "He had to do so much remodeling at Java Jolt after the hurricane, would have been a good time to add a hidden safe or something."

George is hinting for more information.

Morehouse did not oblige. Instead, he asked, "Tiffany talk to the Darth Vadar guy?"

"She tried to," George said. "He just breathed at her. She thinks he had on some kind of platform shoes, so he's not as tall as he looked. She guesses less than six feet, but not a lot less."

"Good," Morehouse said, and looked at Dana. "Tell the others to reduce the height on the guy we're looking for."

I added, "I didn't see the pig until near the end. When he handed me the note. He isn't tall, short actually." I suppressed the ridiculous urge to say I couldn't see the color of the pig's eyes.

"A man for sure?" Morehouse asked.

"Oh." I thought for a few seconds. "Maybe not. He, the person, was very thin and had on some kind of leggings."

Morehouse turned to Renée. "I don't want to traumatize your daughter more, but I need to ask her a couple of questions." He looked from Renée to Andrew. "Why don't the three of us go to Madge's place? Michelle knows it, right?"

"Of course," Aunt Madge said.

As Madge and Renée gathered their purses I turned to Julia. "How about staying here for a bit longer?"

Julia didn't look happy about it, but she nodded. "The dogs make me sneeze."

Scoobie stood and reached for her hand. "C'mon. I'll show you where Pebbles hides."

"She really can't stink up, right?" Julia asked.

I didn't hear Scoobie's response as they entered the bedroom. I wanted to know what Michelle said, but now that I knew she was okay, I wanted most of the people here to leave. My stomach was in knots and I needed to just sit. And maybe have some of the tea Aunt Madge had started to fix.

I could hear the police cars pulling away, and Dana said, "I'll stay a couple of minutes."

"Sure, but, uh, wouldn't you be better with Michelle?"

She smiled. "Morehouse spends a lot of time with his nephews. They're pretty young, and I hear he's good with them."

That made me feel better, and I gestured to the couch. We sat next to each other. George sat across from us, and I could hear Scoobie and Julia in the bedroom.

Dana looked at George. He said, "I won't say a word to Tiffany."

"Good. Since you two worked with Joe most, I have some questions." She leaned into the back of the couch. "First, do either of you have an idea where Joe would go?"

I shook my head slowly. "Because of Tiffany's article mentioning Kansas, I asked him about it."

"Me, too," George said. He looked at me. "Did he give you the line about most of the time in Kansas City?"

Dana cleared her throat. "It would be better if you answered me directly."

Before I could respond, Scoobie walked in, Julia's hand firmly clasped in his. "Just like CSI," he said. "Julia and I are going to drive down to the boardwalk to see if the candy apple lady is still open."

Dana glanced at her watch. "You've got time. She's open 'til six on the weekends."

Julia gave Dana a look that was either questioning or apprehensive.

Dana smiled. "You're always safe with Scoobie."

Julia smiled, but she still didn't let go of Scoobie's hand. I mouthed *thank you* to him and he crossed his eyes at me.

When the door shut behind them, I said, "Joe said he mostly was in Kansas City, and worked day-labor type jobs. After he came back to work at Java Jolt a few hours a day, I asked him where he got the money to start the shop. He looked like he wanted to fire me, but he had that sling, so he needed me."

"And he said?" Dana asked.

"Didn't," George said.

"Maybe not to you. I probably asked more politely." I thought back to the conversation with Joe. "Basically, he said he needed work and he liked the beach. He came here in early spring four years ago. He worked two jobs, slept on the beach, and saved almost all he earned. He said he brought a little with him, but didn't say how much that was."

Dana nodded. "Heard that version the second time we questioned him after the shooting. We didn't ask him to explain where he got his money, but that was kind of the point of asking him about his life when he got here."

I need to tell them about the note. If I didn't, the police could hear it from Scoobie or George. But maybe it wouldn't come up. *Dream on.*

Instead of confessing to my lack of candor, I asked, "Did you know about his other name?"

Dana's tone was sharp. "What other name?"

I swallowed. "On the papers he filed for Java Jolt's New Jersey business license. The name on the application was James Rosen." When I saw her expression, I was glad I told this to Dana rather than Morehouse. "Sorry. I assumed you looked at that."

Before Dana could say anything, George added, "I looked that up, too. Internet. I thought it was like an accountant who filed the papers for him or something."

"Oh, I guess it could have been," I said.

"I'll check," Dana said, dryly. "Probably someone else in the department knows the name."

"Dana." She looked at me. "I'm exhausted. I guess because it was Michelle..."

"Sure." She stood. "Mr. Insurance Investigator can come down to Java Jolt with me to see if things look out of place."

As George shut the door, I heard him ask, "So where was the money?"

I wandered into the kitchen in search of tea, but it was cold, and I really l didn't have a taste for it. With a tall glass of ice water in hand, I went into the bedroom, took a sip, and sat on the edge of the bed. *How would anyone have known to take Michelle? I didn't even know they were coming until a few hours before.*

My pillow looked inviting, so I plopped my head on it and rolled on my side.

"JOLIE? YOU OKAY?"

I registered that Scoobie's voice sounded concerned even before I opened my eyes. "Gosh, I didn't mean to fall asleep. Where are they?" I sat up halfway and he turned on the table lamp.

"If you mean your family, they called my mobile and met Julia and me on the boardwalk." Scoobie sat on the edge of the bed. "Renée was worried when you didn't answer the phone, but I told her George was with you."

I lay back down and stared at the ceiling before I looked at Scoobie again. "He went to Java Jolt with Dana. How was Andrew?"

"Furious, but keeping it under control. Do you think he blames you?"

"Hard to tell, but something Renée said made me think he didn't want them to come down today."

"What?" Scoobie asked.

"He asked her what kind of 'element' would be at the party. When he heard it was at the country club it was okay with him."

"Hmm. Well, he cares about his kids." He grinned. "Maybe he thought the 'element' would all be like me."

I gave him a playful slap on the arm. "He knows you aren't Mr. Pot Smoker now. He likes you."

Scoobie nodded, and then his expression grew serious. "Why didn't you wait for me? Or George? He saw the note with you."

"All I could think about was Michelle. George said...hey. He said he was going to tell Renée Michelle and I went to the ladies room."

"He did for five seconds. She can get stuff out of people faster than Aunt Madge."

I looked at him. "I'm sorry. I just...ran. They said go to Java Jolt."

Scoobie nodded. "It took a couple of minutes for George to get me out of my costume. Geez. I was supposed to call Dr. Welby and tell him what happened to you and Michelle. I'll do that in a few minutes."

"You told him she was gone?"

"He's the one who got Julia to calm down. Renée was good, but the kid freaked."

I closed my eyes. "She said it was the Darth Vadar guy, but we don't know much besides that, do we?"

"No. When I called the police from the car I said that made sense to me, because he was by the door. I'm surprised she went with him though."

My mind played the scene in the country club. "I watched him with the kids. If he grabbed her and turned around fast, no one would have noticed. Everyone was looking at the piñata."

Scoobie nodded. "Scary thought. She was kind of at the edge of the crowd, not too far from where he was standing."

I put my head back on the pillow, and Scoobie looked at me. "You okay?"

"Yes, just really tired."

"I'll make us some soup." He kissed my cheek, stood, and walked toward the kitchen.

As I closed my eyes I wondered who had finally hit the piñata.

CHAPTER EIGHTEEN

WHEN I WOKE UP IT was daylight, and I had decided to find Joe Regan so I could kill him before the police found him.

A note from Scoobie was taped to the lamp shade by our bed. "Had to go to work. Dr. Welby says call him if you need anything."

The house phone rang in the living room, and I stumbled to it.

Aunt Madge sounded worried. "Scoobie phoned me when he left for work. I do have several guests here, but you're welcome to stay over here today."

"That sounds...possible. Maybe for lunch. Do you have plans?"

"Nothing, really. I'll call Harry at the office and he can join us."

"Nuts, I should call him to..."

"He said the new appraisal requests can wait until tomorrow."

"Love you," I said. We hung up and I looked around the house. Everything looked so normal. I didn't feel normal.

In the kitchen, the *Ocean Alley Press* was placed on the table so I'd see the front page article. Not that I could have missed it.

Kidnapping Related to Previous Shooting

A six-year old girl is back with her family after being kidnapped from the Ocean Alley Country Club while attending a Halloween party there yesterday.

The kidnapper, whose identity is unknown because he was in a Darth Vadar costume, wanted cash that was in the possession of Java Jolt owner Joe Regan. A frantic Jolie Gentil, aunt of the six-year old, was able to secure the money and provide it to the kidnappers, who freed the child. There is also no description of the accomplice, who wore a pig costume.

Local police say Regan may have acquired a substantial sum of cash illicitly, while living in Kansas. However, Lieutenant Tortino said, "We are not able to speculate on actions that occurred elsewhere."

Tortino said that Ocean Alley Police believe Regan was shot almost two weeks ago because someone, possibly the kidnappers, wanted the cash, which was hidden in Java Jolt. Regan previously maintained that he had not been involved in any crimes before moving here from Kansas. No law enforcement agency had reported any illicit activity related to Regan.

Regan has been recovering from chest injuries and a broken arm, a result of the shooting, which occurred on Seashore Street two weeks ago. Java Jolt has been operated by several friends of his, though Regan had improved enough to spend brief time at the store in days prior to the kidnapping.

As of press time, Ocean Alley Police had not located the kidnappers or Regan, and police were working with agents from the FBI's Trenton office to try to identify the kidnappers.

The County Club issued a statement noting that Harvest for All Food Pantry hosted the event and was responsible for its attendees.

The *Ocean Alley Press* does not identify minors who are victims of crimes.

Why did they have to identify me? And say it was my niece Darth Vadar kidnapped?

I sat at the kitchen table and let my head fall onto the paper. *So much for Dr. Welby's idea of having a fundraiser in a swanky place.* I started to giggle and couldn't stop.

After a minute I stood and went to the sink to splash water on my eyes. As I dried my face my eyes fell on a note Scoobie had left on the kitchen counter. "Call Renée."

That made me teary. *Stop it, you almost never cry.*

I took a couple of deep breaths and dug in my purse for my mobile phone. I had just dumped all the contents of my purse on the dinette table when I remembered I had dropped my phone in Java Jolt. I looked at the mess on the table and spotted Joe's phone under a wad of tissues. I had forgotten I had it. I wondered why the police hadn't asked me about it, but remembered they didn't know that Joe had given it to me.

I started to push the recent call button, but the house phone rang and I stuffed the phone back in my purse. Caller ID said Renée.

I answered and asked, "Is Michelle okay?"

"She will be. Tell me how you are."

"Uh huh. You first."

Renée was silent for a second, then said, "She won't talk about it. It was hard for her to fall asleep last night, and she asked Andrew several times to be sure the doors were locked. He finally said he'd sleep in the hall outside her bedroom. That let her give in to her total exhaustion."

"I'm sorry, Renée. If I'd had the vaguest notion..."

"It's not your fault. We've got an appointment this afternoon with a child psychologist. Actually, she does. He said he can help her best if they speak alone initially. With our permission. He said to make that clear to her."

"Can I...do anything? Babysit for Julia or something?"

I could almost see Renée shake her head. "She'll be with her best friend, at that girl's house. The mom will be home. Julia has been terrific with Michelle."

"Was Sergeant Morehouse okay with Michelle?"

"Yes. Aunt Madge gave them milk and cookies to share while they talked. He showed her pictures of two little boys before they started to discuss what happened. She wanted to hold them, so she kept his wallet the whole time they talked."

I sighed in relief. "I'm so glad he was good with her."

"Lieutenant Tortino came, too, but he didn't say much. Isn't he the one who marched you off the boardwalk one night because you were smoking?"

"Yes. I didn't know I didn't have to go with him. Aunt Madge grounded me for...I don't remember. Doesn't matter." *I can't believe we're talking about this.*

"Listen, Jolie, we think it would be good, just for a few days, for you not to be with Michelle. You usually aren't, of course..." her voice trailed off.

"Oh, sure. Is, uh, Andrew really angry?"

"It's not so much that. We don't want her to have any reminders of what happened. But if you need to talk, we can meet for lunch or something."

"I'm okay. Did you coordinate with Aunt Madge?"

"A bit. I'm so glad you're with Scoobie."

At that, I smiled. "Me, too."

The phone beeped and I saw 'unknown' on the caller ID. That probably meant the Ocean Alley Police. "Renée, I have to take this call." I disconnected and brought up the new caller.

"Jolie?" It was Dana. When I said yes, she continued. "Are you okay enough to come down to the station? We want you to look at some photos."

"Sure. Give me an hour. I haven't showered or eaten."

AT LEAST I felt rested. The police had asked everyone at the Halloween Party to give them their cameras' SIM cards. Most people were willing to lend them to the police for a few days, but several would not. Dana told me that eventually an officer with a laptop had gone to the country club and downloaded just the Halloween photos and the last attendees had gone home.

I forced myself to focus on the hundreds of photos that were arrayed on the station's conference room table. Any that had Darth Vadar were grouped together in the lower left corner. There were many, since the costume had been such a good one and he'd let kids be enveloped in the cape. There was only one of the pig, and it was from the back. It appeared he really had been there only to give me the note.

I stared at the pig. Man or woman? The person was slim through the hips. Could be either. Something else occurred to me. *Where is a photo of the striped cat?* I slid photos around the table, and eventually found a picture that showed the striped cat handing the popcorn ball to Michelle. I hadn't thought about it at the time, but there weren't popcorn balls on the serving tables. It had to relate to the kidnapping. But how?

It was hard to believe that such a fun day had taken a terrible turn. *It wasn't your fault. All you did was help Joe when he got shot.*

Someone knocked lightly on the door jamb, and Sgt. Morehouse walked in. Before he spoke, I said, "Thanks so much for how you dealt with Michelle."

"So far, you're the only one in your family who ticks me off."

When I smiled, he asked, "Anything jump out at you besides what we talked about yesterday?"

"Nothing about Darth Vadar. His gloves were so long you can't even see his skin color."

Morehouse nodded. "And he never took off his gloves, as far as we've heard. We dusted all over the men's room, too, but there are dozens of different prints. Probably not one will be in the system, unless some esteemed club member had a DUI."

I pointed at the photo of the cat, and found the one of the pig's back. "Look at these, sergeant. Do you think these could be the same person?"

Morehouse stood next to me and stared at them. "Same height. Person favors paper maché heads. You think they're the same?"

"Similar leggings, too." I explained about the popcorn ball not being our treat, and that it seemed odd that someone would single out Michelle.

He tapped the photo of the cat. "Could be a man or a woman. Might have been a way to put Michelle at ease so she'd go with them. Say anything?"

"Just a kind of squeak. Said something about the popcorn ball. He...oh, there might be fingerprints on the plastic wrap."

Morehouse turned sharply and walked out. I stared at the photos for the two minutes it took him to return.

"We gave 'em permission to clean the place last night about eight. I asked the club manager to check their dumpster to see if it's been emptied today."

"That probably thrilled the manager."

"I don't think you'll be invited back," Morehouse said. He tapped the eraser end of a pencil on the table. "When we dusted Joe's apartment, a bunch of your prints showed up."

"Didn't Mrs. Hardy tell you I did an appraisal visit?"

"She did. Prints were mostly on the kitchen counter and some light switches. Notice anything out of the ordinary?"

You mean besides the note with the threat to kill him? "It was really neat, almost no personal items lying around." I thought for a moment. "Harry can give you the pictures I took. I erased them from my camera after I put them on the office computer."

"He already printed them for us. You didn't look in any drawers, open any cabinets?"

I tried to look offended. "An appraiser does not snoop."

"Yeah, Mrs. Hardy said she was always with you."

If she didn't mention I went back by myself, I won't. I gestured at the table of photos. "If these pictures tell you nothing, does that mean you don't know squat about all this?"

Morehouse gave me one of his I-wish-I-never-met-you looks. "You get a good look at the money when you spilled it on the floor at Java Jolt?"

"I didn't spill it, the bag ripped."

"Whatever. Describe the bills."

I frowned, trying to remember. "Wrapped, some in rubber bands, some in little plastic bags. Like for sandwiches. They didn't all look brand new, if that's what you mean."

"Denominations?"

"Mostly I remember fifties and hundreds on the top, and I guess bottom of the bundles, too. Some bundles had twenties, maybe. But I honestly didn't pay much attention."

"How heavy was your coffee can thing? When the money was in it."

"Gee, I dunno. About like Jazz," I said, still thinking.

"As I remember, that cat of yours is pretty small."

"She is, let's see. Oh. It weighed kind of a little more than a three-and-a-half pound bag of cat food. Maybe four pounds."

Morehouse made a note.

"My turn."

"You wish," Morehouse said.

"Fair is fair. Was that from some kind of robbery in Kansas?"

"Likely, but that stolen money wasn't new, so no sequential serial numbers."

"Some numbers?"

He shook his head. "I don't know if the guys were smart or lucky. There were bazaars at three of the churches in town the weekend before. The churches had just brought in a ton of cash that morning."

I thought for a moment. "Wouldn't that have been mostly smaller bills?"

"Very smart, Sherlock. Joe coulda traded 'em in now and then, for larger bills."

"People are more likely to trade for smaller bills at a bank."

Morehouse looked amused. "True. But Joe coulda been switching out small bills with larger ones from his register."

I thought for a moment. "You know, he accepted fifties. A lot of boardwalk businesses don't accept bills over a twenty

"Yeah," Morehouse said, "and he was willing to break large bills for a couple businesses near him. Not often, but some."

"I'd like to give him a big piece of my mind."

Morehouse shook a finger at me. "Keep it. Joe's apparent partner did a couple of armed robberies, but it looks like this mighta been Joe's first offense, of any kind. But he'll feel cornered now. He's gotta be long gone, but if you see him, stay away from him."

I reached for my purse. "I know, call you..hey. What about the other name on Joe's business forms? The ones he filed with the state."

"How the hell did you know that?"

"I can read." When he stared at me, I said, "The forms are public information."

"Which you didn't have any need to see."

I stared at Morehouse.

He frowned. "You know, everybody thinks this online crap is so good. It ain't all good. James Rosen is nobody we can find. Joe musta put in a fake name in case his own popped up in connection with the robbery. That form was the only legal document we can find for him here. He never transferred his driver's license, and it'd been expired for a year."

"Don't they check or something when you do those forms?"

"You gotta send in a scan of your driver's license. But he had a fake one. His Kansas one with the James Rosen name stripped in. Nobody checks that crap."

Morehouse's phone buzzed and he answered it. "How long ago? Hmm. How many bags? Yeah. If it's searched it won't be you." He hung up.

At least I'm not the only one he hangs up on.

"Dumpster's been emptied. Somebody coulda eaten the popcorn thing, and there's probably hundreds of pieces of plastic wrap stuff. I doubt we'll go to the landfill to sift fifty bags of trash."

"Oh. Well, she's found, so it's not like you need the prints to get a child back."

He eyed me. "Don't you have to be somewhere?"

I wanted to know one more thing. "If you think Darth Vadar might be the guy who went to prison after the robbery, do you have a photo of that guy?"

"For what?"

"Maybe I've seen him around." I really hoped it wasn't Talbot Peters, but I wanted to see the guy's face.

From the folder he was carrying, Morehouse pulled a photo. "Taken when the guy started parole."

The man had a couple of days of stubble, but no handlebar mustache or goatee. The face was fuller than the one taken at the time of the robbery. The man in the picture was serious rather than sullen. Green eyes, so the violet eyes must be contact lenses. He didn't have Talbot Peters' styled hair or big smile, but I felt confident the photo was Peters.

"Did George talk to you about a guy named Talbot Peters?"

MOREHOUSE ACCUSED me of deliberately not telling him I thought Peters was someone Joe knew. I denied it, but he said the FBI or U.S. Marshals, who had been looking for Belken, might want to talk to me. *Just what I need.*

I walked to my car. If Morehouse was angry that I didn't suggest Peters could be Belken, how much trouble could I be in for not telling Morehouse about the death threat? I still didn't want to confess to that earlier lack of candor.

Part of me was grateful that Joe had given me the money to exchange for Michelle. He could have kept lying about having it. Another part still wanted to find Joe before the police did so I could get in one good punch before he got arrested. And still another part wanted all of this to just go away.

What about the pig's threat? And who was the pig? It could have been Belken's old girlfriend. I thought an article said he might have forced her to go with him. It seemed as if she could have found a way to escape him, but I'd read plenty of articles about abducted people cowed into submission even when away from their kidnapper.

Could Joe be with Darth Vadar and the pig? Joe had been in Java Jolt when I'd run out. The pig and his Darth Vadar buddy would have been running away from Ocean Alley, but there was no indication that Joe went with them when he left Java Jolt. And how did he do that? He was in bad shape. He couldn't exactly flag a cab. Not that there are many in Ocean Alley in the off-season.

I flexed the fingers on my right hand. Supposedly hitting people hurt. I should probably drop the idea of punching Joe.

A glance at the clock on my dashboard said I should head to Aunt Madge's for lunch. But one thing couldn't wait. I pulled out Joe's phone, turned it on, and scrolled through his contacts list. I knew almost everyone. The few who were not

Ocean Alley people had identities like "bulk coffee" and "cheap cleaning."

I switched to the recent call list. Mostly known quantities, but there were two calls from people who weren't in his contact list, so weren't identified by name. I didn't recognize the area code, but if it was the kidnappers they'd have burner phones, as Scoobie called them.

Still, I jotted the numbers on the back of a grocery receipt in my purse. I'd have to give the phone to Morehouse, but that didn't mean I couldn't...Wait. Joe could have my phone. If the police had found it on the floor at Java Jolt, they would have said so. Maybe even given it back to me.

I dialed my number. Someone picked up, but said nothing.

"Joe?"

"Damn," he said.

"Where are you?"

"Can't say." He coughed. "If you haven't given it to the police, please toss the phone."

"I have to give it to them."

He didn't say anything for a few seconds, and then asked, "Your niece okay?"

I felt my irritation growing. "She wouldn't have been kidnapped if you'd given the guys the money."

His laugh was ragged, and ended with a cough. "I'da been dead as soon as I handed it to them."

"What, you thought they'd go away?"

"Thought they might get caught. I called in," he coughed again, "a tip to Kansas parole."

"Why are you coughing?"

"Broken rib, I think." He paused. "You really won't toss it?"

"Why? What's on it?"

"Just a couple of calls that show he called me."

"I don't think people doubt that now." It was my turn to pause. "You need a doctor. Where are you?"

"You gotta let go of this, Jolie. The kid's safe."

I started to say I wanted my phone, but he'd hung up.

Who was *he?*

CHAPTER NINETEEN

AFTER LUNCH WITH Aunt Madge and Harry and going home to feed Jazz and Pebbles, I headed for the police station. My plan was to tell Morehouse I had just found the phone in my purse, and forgotten I didn't have mine. He'd yell, but that would be over in a few minutes.

When I got to Main Street near the police station, the street was blocked and a patrol officer motioned my car onto F Street. I pushed my window down and called to him as I got closer. "What's up?"

"Just keep...Jolie?"

The officer looked somewhat familiar, but I couldn't remember why, and I couldn't see his name badge.

"Morehouse is looking for you." He pointed to the edge of the group of sawhorses that blocked most of the street. Only a small car could pass through.

I pushed the button to raise my car widow, but it didn't budge. "Damn."

"Now what?" he asked.

I pushed the button a few more times. "My car window won't go up. I just got the car back after it got rammed a couple of weeks ago."

"Yeah, that was a good day for you. Keep moving," he said.

Irritated, I drove around the barricade and pulled into the police station parking lot. Black sedans and SUVs took up all the parking spaces, and a couple were parked behind police cars, blocking them into their spots. I stopped.

I pushed the button to roll up my window, again with no success. *So much for a repaired car.* A man in a suit walked toward me. He was maybe thirty, with close-cropped black hair and a waterproof jacket that said FBI on the front.

"Why'd he point you here?" he asked.

"He said Sergeant Morehouse was looking for me."

"I got it." Morehouse walked toward us. His shoulder holster was on the outside of his sports jacket, and he was perspiring even on such a cool day. He pointed at me. "Stay in your car."

"What? What is it?" I asked.

"We think Regan might be around here. His phone was just used in this area."

Uh oh.

IT WAS MORE than a little bit of yelling.

"I was bringing it back! I told you, I just realized I had it."

We were in the small conference room in the police station. Sergeant Morehouse, Lieutenant Tortino, Captain Edwards, and two very angry FBI agents were staring at me.

"That's crap," Morehouse said. "You used the phone."

"I thought somebody had mine. Maybe even Joe."

The FBI agent's tone was more modulated, but no less angry. "Why would Mr. Regan have your phone?"

I explained how mine had fallen to the floor in Java Jolt, and that I had to take Joe's because the kidnappers were supposed to call me on it. "I figured if you had my phone you'd have given it to me. So I called it to see who had it."

Tortino's tone was as aggravated as Morehouse's. "And you had to use Regan's phone? You couldn't use any other phone in town?"

I shrugged. "I'd just found it in the bottom of my purse. I didn't think about it."

"You used it forty-five minutes ago," the FBI agent said. "Why didn't you bring it right here? Did you go to see Mr. Regan?"

"Get real," I said.

"This is damn serious, Jolie," Tortino said.

"I was supposed to have lunch with Aunt Madge. I didn't want her to be irritated if I was late."

"And you'd rather have local and federal law enforcement angry with you?" the agent asked.

"Well, kind of."

Morehouse ran his fingers through his very short hair. "Did Joe say where he was?"

"No, he just asked me to throw away the phone."

The FBI agent started to say something, but I asked, "Can't you sort of trace my phone to see where it was when he answered it?"

"I have people on it." The FBI agent stood and left the room. I didn't even remember his name. The second agent stood, looked at me directly, and walked out. Apparently I was to be left to the local police.

I looked at Morehouse. "That guy's grouchy."

Morehouse turned red. "Dammit, Jolie..."

Captain Edwards cut him off. "Jolie, by holding onto that phone as long as you did, you could be arrested for obstructing an FBI investigation."

"But I only remembered I had it a little while ago!"

He raised his voice. "And they still might. They're the ones handling the kidnapping investigation. I suggest you go about your normal day. Do not, and I mean do not, look for Joe or your phone."

"Yes, sir." *Arrested? No way.*

The captain stood. He's easily the tallest cop in town, and dresses like a Wall Street banker. "I mean it. I don't want to see you in here again." He left the room.

Morehouse's face wasn't red any more. "That goes double for me." He and Tortino stood and left.

I sat at the table for another fifteen or twenty seconds and wondered if Dana would tell me if the fingerprints in Java Jolt the day Joe got shot were the same as those on the steering wheel of the car whose driver ran away. And where my phone was when Joe answered it.

SCOOBIE WAS AT work, and he wouldn't want to talk about Joe's whereabouts even if he wasn't. Except maybe to tell me not to delve into it. That left George. With my car window still down, I headed for Java Jolt. George had said he would talk the building owner into letting him keep the coffee shop open. Because the landlord knew Joe had given George the go-ahead to run it temporarily, George expected permission to take over the lease, at least in the short term. I figured the landlord wanted the space occupied.

When George saw me his face lit up and he began to take off his apron. I shook my head, and walked behind the service counter.

He motioned me into the hallway. "Listen, Jolie, Joe may be somewhere downtown. I want to..."

"He isn't. At least he's not where all the police activity was." As I told him about the calamity my phone call to Joe had caused, I could tell he wanted to lambast me for not calling him. I ended by saying, "And Morehouse, even Captain Edwards, are furious with me. Be glad you weren't involved in any of it."

George frowned. "So, if your phone was within range of a tower near here they might find out quickly. Otherwise it'll take awhile."

"It only took a few minutes to track Joe's phone to the parking lot."

"Yes, but some FBI computer geek had already programmed their system to set off an alert when that phone was used."

"Oh, like TV."

"So," George took off his apron, "that's why you need to mind Java Jolt for maybe an hour while I go snoop at the courthouse or police station."

"I've never been here alone!"

"Relax, it's the slowest time of day."

I WAS MOPPING coffee off the floor when George came back forty-five minutes later.

"What happened?" George's eyes swept Java Jolt, taking in that there were no customers at the moment.

No way to avoid telling him. Three regular customers were in the shop when I forgot to put the coffee pot for decaf under the brewing machine. Someone would rat me out. "The decaf coffee didn't aim right."

He opened his mouth to say something, shut it, and then must have decided on a safer topic. "The prints on the car that someone deserted the day Joe got shot, some were the same as the ones on the Java Jolt door that morning. But only on the car's door handle and turn signal. It's like he wiped and missed a couple of prints."

I squeezed the sponge mop into the trash can.

"Why are you...?" George began.

"Because I don't feel like walking back to the sink in the hall, and the sink out here can only be used for making coffee and washing hands."

"Did you hear what I said?" George asked.

I leaned on the mop stick. "It means whoever scared Joe enough to leave the shop hotwired a car and crashed it in front of Mr. Markle's store. After the crash, he ran off, but not too far. He was near the grocery store when Joe left it."

"Huh, you do listen. Maybe saw him go in there and hung around until he came out," George mused. "But you didn't see anyone when he got shot."

"Nope." I walked toward the hall to put the mop away, but stopped. "Who told you?"

"I saw Dana in Burger King..."

"You left me here to go to..."

"Geez, keep your cool. I saw her go in so I followed her. She said since it was your idea to compare the prints, she was passing it on. If you or I tell anyone she told us, we'll get a traffic ticket once a month for the rest of our lives."

"We have to tell Scoobie," I said. "But you better do it so he doesn't know I asked her about the prints."

George almost sputtered. "You said you'd tell him what you, we were doing."

I shrugged. "I give him the big picture."

George had something to say about that, but two customers came in, so he couldn't. I left before he could try to find out what I was or wasn't telling Scoobie.

AS I GOT IN my car I cursed whoever rammed me. I wasn't up for taking the car back in today. Luckily it wasn't raining.

I didn't have a way to find out where Joe had been when he answered my phone, but it didn't seem as if there could be too many options. A guy with a sling and a beat-up face does not blend in with people taking a stroll on the boardwalk.

To help me think of his possibilities, I drove up C Street toward the northern end of Ocean Alley. There were probably two hundred summer cottages that were vacant in the off-season. But Joe would need food and water. And an ice pack for his eye, but at this point that was a luxury.

After going about half a mile, two police cars blocked the road, lights flashing. *This must be the area where Joe answered my phone.*

I turned left, intending to go back to my house. The route took me by Mrs. Hardy's house. *I bet she didn't expect a criminal for a tenant.*

"Wait a minute." I pulled to the curb one house down from hers. Joe probably had a key to the apartment. Whether he had it with him was something else. Mrs. Hardy had her routine, he'd know when it was safe to sneak in. Or he could wait until nightfall. However, since he might have left his hiding place after I called him, he would not have had a dark night to conceal him. He might have gone into the apartment in daylight.

It was worth a shot. I got out of the car and locked it. Not that it mattered with a window down.

Mrs. Hardy answered her door after I knocked twice. She looked irritated, but her expression cleared somewhat when she saw me. "Jolie. This is a surprise."

With a broad smile, I told her I wanted to chat about whether she was happy with her appraisal, or if she had any suggestions for how we could do better.

She unlocked the storm door. "Oh, a customer service call. How nice."

I'm in. How do I get the key?

Mrs. Hardy had been pleased with what the appraisal said her house was worth and how quickly she got the information. What she really wanted to do was talk about the apartment she had found in Silver Times Senior Living, a retirement complex I knew well.

"And they'll paint it before I move in. Doesn't it sound perfect?"

"It does. You'll probably know a lot of the other residents." *The key is on a hook near the kitchen door.*

"Oh, yes. And there are clubs, for bridge and Scrabble and all kinds of things."

I cleared my throat. "Would you mind if I got a drink of water before I go?"

She began to stand, and I smiled. "You stay there. I'll use the cup you served me tea in."

Mrs. Hardy appeared slightly perplexed, but sat back down. I ran the water from the tap for a few seconds as I checked to be sure the key was still on its hook. It was.

When the cup was half full I turned off the water. As I got to the doorway I ran my hand along the frame, snagging the key ring on my pinkie. "Even the wood around the doors is in perfect condition."

She beamed. "Oh yes, my Roger saw to everything."

My left hand stayed at my side as I sat, and I raised the teacup to my mouth with the other hand. "There's nothing like fresh water."

"Certainly not."

We talked for another five minutes, during which time I was able to slide the key into the pocked of my slacks by pretending to look for a tissue. When that was finally accomplished I made to stand. "I know you'll enjoy Silver Times."

"Oh, you need to go? You only just got here."

"My pets need to go out." I let her think I had dogs.

"You never want to delay that!" She laughed.

I drove straight home, arguing with myself the entire way. *He's not up there. He might be up there. You should call the police and suggest they search the apartment. You can't let Captain Edwards think you're meddling. Or Morehouse.*

My bigger internal debate was whether to tell Scoobie what I planned to do. I rationalized that I would afterwards. I thought about having George go with me, but it would look odd enough for one person to walk up the exterior steps. Two would be really suspicious, and George would probably only help me if we told Scoobie in advance.

The best time to go was as soon as Scoobie left for work the next morning. Few people are out at six-thirty in the morning on a November day. It would still be somewhat dark, too.

Why are you doing this? So you can punch Joe. You decided that would hurt your hand. Okay, I'll kick him in his bad arm. Who are you kidding? You aren't some martial arts guru.

The latter point was certainly true. I told myself I was going for two reasons. First, I hate loose ends, have since I was a teenager. Second, if Joe could be persuaded to go to the police, he would get a much lighter sentence for whatever he'd done than if he was brought in from hiding. *What do you care? He didn't have to give you the money for Michelle.*

As I got home, Scoobie's car pulled in next to mine in our small driveway. He looked irritated.

We both got out of our cars. "What? You look mad. You don't get mad."

"I don't like to be angry," he said. "Tell me it isn't true."

The expression on my face told him I didn't know what he was talking about. "You didn't keep Joe's phone overnight, did you?"

I almost blurted that that was a few hours ago, and I was on to something else. Thankfully, I stopped before that came out. "I honestly didn't remember that I had it." We were on the porch by now, and Scoobie put his key in the lock. "Mine fell on the floor at Java Jolt, remember?"

"Yes. That part I'm clear on."

Gee, he's really angry. "Joe's phone is much smaller, it was at the bottom of my purse. With everything that went on, well, I plain didn't think of it."

I bent to pick up Jazz, and for a second felt mildly dizzy. "I drove it to the police station myself, almost as soon as I found it."

"So you didn't call Joe?"

"Gee whiz. How does stuff get around so fast?"

Scoobie had continued to stand as I sat on the couch. His expression radiated exasperation. "You really did?"

"I wasn't calling Joe. I called my phone to see where it was, who had it. It's not my fault that he answered."

"I need to check my email." He turned abruptly and walked into the guest bedroom.

I put Jazz on the floor and sat, stunned. Scoobie was really angry with me. So angry he wouldn't talk about it. At least, not right now. I considered following him into the guest room, but if there's one thing I learned in All-Anon, it's that I'm not responsible for how someone feels. *Well, maybe now.*

It didn't matter how logical it might be to let Scoobie deal with his emotions himself, it didn't feel right. I stood, intending to talk to him, but he came out of the room.

Saying nothing, he pulled his jacket off the back of the chair he had just placed it on, and said, "I'm going out for a bit. Back about nine."

"Okay." Nine o'clock? Where would he be for that long? AA or Narcotics Anonymous meetings didn't start for more than two hours, and they were over long before nine.

I was literally pacing a path around the living room, into the larger bedroom, and back when something occurred to me. It would be dark by about six-thirty this evening. I could check on Joe's apartment today. No need to wait for morning. Once I did that, especially if he was there and agreed to go to the police with me, all of this would be over.

CHAPTER TWENTY

I WAITED UNTIL about six-forty-five, when it was fully dark. It was the coldest night of the season so far, but was still above freezing. I pulled a heavier navy blue coat from the closet and checked the pocket for gloves. I didn't bother with a hat.

After driving by Mrs. Hardy's house twice, I figured she was watching television in the living room, with blinds and curtains closed. I parked at the house next door, which let me get to the exterior stairs without having to walk by her front door.

Instinct said I should walk up the stairs on tip-toe, but that doesn't work well when you have on running shoes that have a thick sole. I settled for creeping, constantly looking around for someone who would snitch on me.

The lack of a storm door on the upstairs apartment meant one less entry point that could creak. The key was in my hand and I gently inserted it into the lock on the door handle and turned it. The knob rotated easily. I pushed open the door, walked in, and shut it behind me.

"Joe?"

"What the hell, Jolie?"

Oh boy, now what?

"Is anyone with you?"

"No." I followed Joe's voice to the bedroom. He was lying on the floor of the closet, which was about seven feet long and had pocket doors, which were open. There were jackets and slacks hanging above him. Joe didn't look good. From my purse I took a small bottle of water and a cheese sandwich. He almost inhaled the sandwich.

Joe lay back, and stared at the closet ceiling. He turned to me. "Why are you here?"

"You didn't have to give me the money for Michelle." I tried to get a better look at his face, but the only light was from a street lamp just outside the bedroom window. "I want to help you. Let me drive you to the police, or a hospital and they can call…"

"No!" Joe shut his eyes. "I had no idea they would do anything like kidnap a kid. I was holding onto the money because I knew he'd kill me as soon as I gave it to him. Kind of counting on his Kansas parole people to look for him here. They got that anonymous tip."

"He would have been back."

Joe nodded. "Probably, but I'd have been gone by then. Next place I go, I don't open a business."

"That's how they found you?"

"So they say. I put a different name on the business filing because I thought that would be an easy database to search. But it was too complicated to officially change my name or get forged documents, and they eventually found me with a Google search." He paused for breath. "Can you believe that?"

I shrugged. "That's how I found Belken's name."

"Crap."

"Joe, you can't stay here like this. A broken rib can puncture a lung. You should know all about that."

His smile was grim. "Yeah. But I don't want to go to prison. Or run into Belken."

"What exactly did you do?"

He looked at me.

"I'm not the police."

"You also aren't my wife. They can compel anyone except a spouse to spill their guts."

"Ah. How about if I tell you what I pieced together?"

He didn't answer.

"It looks to me as if you were supposed to be Belken's ride the day of the robbery, but someone in the bank tripped a silent alarm. You drove off, and Belken made it out with a bunch of cash. By the time the police picked him up, he'd ditched the cash. You left town with it."

Joe said nothing.

"What I can't figure is why he didn't name you, to help him get a reduced sentence."

"Without saying we're talking about me, Belken probably thought if he kept quiet he could get at the money later. But when he got out, he...couldn't."

"So basically, this person who isn't you stole money from a crook."

"If the person's partner hadn't been such a violent person, he might have turned it in. All he wanted was to get away. Even as desperate as I was, I shouldn't have agreed to drive the car. I mean, the guy shouldn't have agreed."

"Then why do it?"

He grimaced. "Lost two jobs during the recession. Bank took the guy's house."

"Hmm. I'm no lawyer, but there wasn't any kind of warrant out for this guy. You never went to jail and didn't bug out on parole, like Belken. You, this guy, could probably negotiate a really small sentence. Maybe not even prison." I had no idea if this was true, but if Belken got three years and he was in the bank with a gun, it didn't seem that Joe would get that much.

Joe shut his eyes again. "The thing is, I've lied to cops here. I knew who shot me."

"Seems like the shooter would be in more trouble."

The voice from the doorway was harsh. "That's probably right."

Talbot Peters was taller than I remembered and no easy smile graced his face tonight. He also had a slight southern accent, more like what I think of as mid-South rather than the strong accent of Mississippi or Alabama. Talbot must have deliberately hidden the drawl when he talked to people in Ocean Alley. Except when Max heard him arguing with Joe.

"How, how did you get in here?" I asked, as my stomach did its version of a back flip. *Did I lock the door? I didn't lock the door!*

Joe came to a full sitting position. He had to hold one hand over his ribs to do it. "Barry, she doesn't know..."

"Talbot," the bank robber said. "I need to be through with Barry Belken. Too many people looking for him."

Joe and I said nothing. Peters spoke again. "You had more money, Joe. Where the hell is it?"

"You need to let Jolie leave. She doesn't need to be here."

"Sure," he sneered. "Let her go so she can call some of her buddies in the police."

Morehouse would not call me his buddy. Especially now. "I could wait an hour, and then make an anonymous call saying a man at this address needs medical care."

Peters' laugh was loud and rough. "Oh, he won't need medical care."

I was suddenly aware that Mrs. Hardy's television must have been turned off. I hadn't registered that I was hearing it up here until it was quiet. She might have heard Peters. *Please let her call the police. Don't let her come up here!*

"Where's Benji?" Joe asked.

"The bitch ran off after we let the kid go."

"Don't hurt Benji, Barry," Joe said.

"Forget her. You got your own problems." Peters drew a gun from his pocket.

"She stood by you, and then she turned her life around. You need to keep away from Benji."

Belken-cum-Talbot gave another harsh laugh. "Benji's always been able to take care of herself."

Almost to myself, I said, "She was the pig."

"Shut up!" Talbot pointed the gun at me and I recoiled.

"Where's the rest of the money, Regan?"

I made an involuntary whimper.

"Shut up!"

I'm not sure I could define a crazed expression, but I recognized one now. And I could do nothing to stop him. I didn't even have a mobile phone. I promised myself that if I got out of this I was going to have at least two of those phones that didn't require a contract. I'd always have a replacement phone.

Joe's voice was raspy. "Peters, listen to me. It's gone. I put it into my business."

"Wrong answer," Peters roared. "Do you know how damned nasty prison is? Always with a bunch of sweaty men. The crappiest food you ever ate. I spent three years there, Joe. I'm going to get paid for that."

"How about some profit-sharing for future years?" Joe asked.

Profit sharing? This isn't a Chamber of Commerce meeting.

"You don't have any future years."

"What if..." I began.

"I told you to shut up!" Peters looked at me and I cringed.

"Get on your feet, Regan. The three of us are taking a ride."

"You have a car?" I asked, hoping to spot a hole in his plan.

"Sometimes. Tonight we're using yours. Going someplace real quiet."

Joe struggled to his feet. I wondered how he'd gotten here. Mrs. Hardy's house was several blocks from the area the police had barricaded on C Street. However, once Joe was on his feet he was steady.

My thoughts raced. He wanted to go someplace quiet to kill us. I had to figure out a way to draw attention to us when we got outside.

Peters waved his gun at me. "You first, girlie."

I walked through the small living room and opened the door that led to the stairs.

"Don't run away now. Wouldn't be a party without you. You wanna party with me later?"

I thought I was going to throw up. Somehow, saying no did not seem a good thing. "Depends on the kind of party."

"Good answer," my captor said.

I was on the top landing. *Why aren't there any cars?* At this time of night, E Street was usually really busy. I'd gone down a few steps when it occurred to me that maybe the police were keeping people off of E Street. Maybe they knew we were here. *Please God, please God.*

A beat-up Ford pick-up turned onto the street. It sounded as if the driver considered a muffler optional equipment. It also meant my hope for a police rescue was probably a pipe dream.

Joe was behind me, and I assumed Peters was after him. I didn't look. *Why am I calling him Peters?*

The pick-up was almost even with the house when three men popped up from the truck bed, each pointing a gun in our direction.

"Put it down, Belken!" It sounded like the FBI agent.

I crouched on the step.

"Stand up, bitch!" Belken roared.

The gunfire was incredibly loud and seemed to go on forever. I had my hands over my ears almost immediately, but it didn't decrease the sound. And the smoke. So much smoke from the guns.

The sound of splintering wood made me look up. Barry Belken was covered in his own blood. Some of it had splashed on Joe, who was sitting on the step behind me.

Belken had let go of his gun, which was clattering down the wooden staircase. His arms were raised and spread out, as if he was a kid about to make an angel print in the snow.

He fell very slowly.

I leaned over the railing and threw up.

CHAPTER TWENTY-ONE

BELKEN WAS DEAD and Joe was in the hospital. I was sitting in the police station, and everyone I ever knew was furious with me. For once, I thought they were right. It was one thing to try to find Joe. It was something else altogether to look for him when the other person hunting for him was a criminal on parole who had a bad temper. *But I didn't know the guy was still in town.*

I was too ashamed to ask Aunt Madge to come to the station, so Scoobie was on my right and George was on the left. Dana had found them at an AA meeting, and they were very unhappy about police coming into a meeting that was supposed to be anonymous.

Morehouse had asked me a question, but I'd been thinking rather than listening.

"Could you repeat that?" I asked.

"Do you realize if Officer Leland hadn't spotted your car we wouldn't have had people there when you left that house?"

"The officer who came to Harry's after someone tried to smash me? He spotted my car?"

"The damn driver's side window was down."

It took a moment for me to associate Officer Leland with my smashed car and the roadblock of earlier in the day. "Oh, I thought Mrs. Hardy must have called."

"She did," Morehouse said. "But we wouldn't have put it together with you and Joe if Leland hadn't just called in your car. He remembered it from the window that wouldn't go up, and knew you shouldn't be near Joe's old apartment."

"I'll have to thank him." I said this with every ounce of meekness I could muster.

"How did you get into that upstairs apartment?"

I swallowed. "I had a key."

His tone implied he was losing patience with me. "Where did you get it?"

"From a hook in Mrs. Hardy's kitchen."

"With her permission?"

"Not that time," I said.

"Great," Scoobie muttered.

"You're in here because she asked for you and until now I didn't think Jolie had committed a crime. You wanna go?"

"I might need to think about that."

Morehouse looked at the pad he took notes on. "I can understand that."

I don't like to be talked about as if I'm not in the room, but it didn't seem the time to mention that.

My heart beat faster. "I wanted..." I began.

George interrupted me. "You maybe shouldn't say anything without a lawyer."

"I haven't Miranda'd you yet," Morehouse said.

Yet?

"And we may not. You can have a lawyer, of course," he finished.

I sat up straighter. "Probably taking the key was the only illegal thing I did. Whatever penalty there is for that, I deserve it."

"Too bad snooping isn't illegal," Scoobie said.

Morehouse looked at him. "Give it a rest."

"You know, I think I'll rest in the waiting area." Scoobie looked at me as he stood. "I'll give you a ride to your house."

He said your house! It's our house.

George seemed to have picked up on this. When Scoobie closed the door after himself, George patted my hand. "He'll work through it."

Tears were starting to make their way down my cheeks, and I brushed my eyes.

One of the FBI agents walked in and sat down, saying nothing. I avoided looking at him.

"So, did Belken come in at the same time, or later?" Morehouse asked.

I sniffed. "I'd say about eight to ten minutes later. I assume he followed me, but maybe he'd been watching the house."

"Not like we'll know," Morehouse said. "What did Joe say to you? About tonight, or anything from the last couple of weeks."

"I can't say he specifically admitted to anything."

Morehouse frowned. "Jolie..."

"I asked him what the heck was going on. He said I wasn't his spouse, so I'd have to tell you anything he said. He, um, thanked me for the cheese sandwich."

"You took him a sandwich?" George asked.

"Shut up, George."

I've heard Morehouse say that to George maybe ten times. "I figured if I found Joe, he'd need it. He was pretty beat up when I saw him in Java Jolt."

"Yeah, cheese is good for a black eye." Morehouse muttered. "That's all he said?"

I thought for a few seconds. "He said something like people like Belken were dangerous. If a guy gave them what they wanted they'd probably kill him. It was better to just get away."

"Gee," Morehouse said, sarcasm evident, "I wonder who he was talking about?"

I shrugged. "He was really careful about what he said. When I suggested he come with me to get help and see you..."

"You said that?" Morehouse asked.

"Well, yes. That's why I was looking for him." I paused. "He didn't have to give me the money for Michelle, you know."

Morehouse just looked at me, and I continued. "He said he had committed one crime. He lied to you. He knew who shot him."

"Did he say who that was?" the FBI agent asked.

I stared at him for a second. "The implication seemed pretty clear, so I didn't ask."

Morehouse wrote a lot in his book, talking as he did so. "Crap. A whole lot of things could have been avoided if he'da told us that from the get-go."

"No kidding," George said, but softly. Morehouse didn't tell him to shut up.

"Oh, one more thing," I said. "Joe said he'd called in an anonymous tip to some Kansas Parole Board. To say Belken was here."

Tortino opened the door and came part-way into the room. "You need a recorder?"

"Fine by me," I said.

Tortino was behind Morehouse, so he shifted to look at him. "Not tonight. Not as much to tell as I thought." He looked at me. "You be prepared to be recorded later. You're pale as a sheet now, so you can go home in a couple of minutes."

If we'd been in Newark or Trenton, I figured I would have been treated very differently. They knew me here, knew I had not committed any crimes with Joe. They might not like me right now, but they believed me.

SCOOBIE DIDN'T SAY ANYTHING as we drove home. When we got in the house, I sat on the couch, exhausted. I'd hoped he would sit next to me, maybe give me a hug, but he sat across from me, in the rocker.

"I don't know where to go with this, Jolie. I'm not sure I can ever trust you again."

I nodded, trying very hard not to cry. Crying wasn't fair. "I don't blame you. Would it help if I said I've really, truly, learned a lesson tonight?"

"Maybe a bit." He shrugged. "You were saved by pure luck tonight. If that cop hadn't seen your car, if Mrs. Hardy didn't have her hearing aids in, I'd be helping Madge and Harry plan a funeral."

I whispered. "I have a lot to be thankful for."

"And I have a lot of thinking to do, and I have to work tomorrow." He stood. "If you're okay, I think I'll bunk with George tonight."

I nodded, but said nothing. He walked into the guest room, which is where he kept his clothes, and I could hear him opening drawers and the closet. When he came out he had a set of scrubs on a hanger and a small duffel bag.

"I'll catch you later." He opened the door and left, saying as he closed it, "Turn on the alarm system."

What have I done? I managed to wait until his car started before lying sideways on the couch and sobbing.

AT FOUR IN THE morning I woke up. Jazz and Pebbles were sitting on the floor in front of the couch, apparently concerned that I was sleeping there instead of in my bed. "Oh, you guys are hungry." I sat up and then stood, stretching. I was stiff from being in such an awkward position. They led me into the kitchen, and each sat by her respective bowl.

That made me smile for a second. "You know Jazz, we've had relationships end before, but this guy's a keeper." I put my face in my hands and sobbed. "What am I going to do?"

Jazz wound her way around my ankles, and after a minute I stopped. "It's no wonder my head is stuffed up."

After putting out food and fresh water for Jazz and Pebbles, I stumbled into the shower. The hot water woke me up some, and I felt better once I had dried my hair and dressed. I wouldn't be able to sleep, and my mind was going full tilt.

For several minutes I walked through the house, occasionally straightening a picture on the wall or making sure my bedspread was tucked in tightly. On the bedside table was the notebook I use to make lists. I picked it up and then grabbed the duvet from the bottom of the bed. After I wrapped it around my shoulders I sat on the couch.

My list of Apologies Needed grew to two pages very quickly. Aunt Madge was first, since I'd known her longer. After that there was no particular order.

Aunt Madge
- Making her worry.
- Embarrassing her.
- Lying by omission

Harry
- Putting the appraisal office in a bad light
- Making him worry.
- Lying by omission

Mrs. Hardy
- Taking her key.
- Lying twice (mail search/key).
- Her porch rail.
- Scaring her

Renée
- Getting Michelle kidnapped.
- Worrying her.
- Probably making Andrew mad at her.

Scoobie
- Everything
- Lying about…

I was so intent on what I was writing that I didn't hear the key in the lock. I looked up as Scoobie came in, already dressed for work.

"What time is it?"

He stared at me. "Just after six. Why are you up?"

"The girls got me up about four. I couldn't go back to sleep."

He turned to leave.

"I'm sorry. About..." I knocked my list on the floor as I tried to stand, "all of it."

He glanced at the pad, but didn't walk over. "We'll talk tonight. I'm honestly not sure what I want to do."

I TURNED ON THE TV, but changed the channel every time a news flash mentioned what some idiot called "coffee gate." The *Ocean Alley Press* plopped onto the porch, but I ignored it.

Someone knocked at about seven-fifteen. I peered out the peephole and then flung it open. "Ramona!"

She looked the same. Her long blonde hair was swept into a large clip and her clothing was the same 1970s-hippie look that she favors and wears well. More important, she was smiling at me. "Heard you put your foot in it."

I stood aside so she could come in, and we hugged. "It's not like you haven't warned me through the years. I'm really glad to see you." I followed her into my living room where she sat on the rocker. "Is your course over?"

Ramona looked around the room. "You have new curtains."

"Special at the thrift store."

She smiled. "It was over yesterday. There's a dinner tonight, but George called and said it might be good to come home now."

"Oh, Ramona, I'm..."

She waved a hand. "I can drive back to Philadelphia later if I want." I had sat on the couch opposite her, and she looked at me intently. "Did Scoobie really leave?"

I'd been trying to hold myself together, but that did it. I leaned over my lap, put my face in my hands, and sobbed. "Yes. Maybe. I'm not sure."

She sat next to me and alternated between patting my shoulder and giving me one-armed hugs. "Shh. It'll be okay."

"You don't know that," I sobbed. "I messed it all up. Why do I always...have to know?"

"You have lots of friends who care about you," she said. "And Aunt Madge, and your sister."

"But I think I lost Scoobie!" I said this at full wail. "And I can't stop crying and my stupid stomach is upset all the time from working at that stupid coffee shop."

She missed a couple of pats. "You usually have a cast-iron stomach. Come on, sit up. I'll make you some tea."

"I hate tea!" I sat up and she was smiling at me.

"Not funny," I sniffed.

"I know. I was trying to figure out what's not stupid or what you don't hate."

I grabbed a tissue from the table next to the couch and blew my nose."

"Probably not much today."

She stood. "The diner is open. If you don't want tea, I'll get you one of Arnie's milkshakes while you wash your face." She made a shooing motion as she picked up her purse. "Go on. Put lipstick on, you'll feel better."

She left and I went to the bathroom to splash water on my face. The mirror was not kind, so I opened the medicine cabinet to look at its contents rather than my face.

Ramona likes tea, so I filled the kettle and turned on the burner. It still didn't seem as if tea would bring its usual comfort. *Nuts. I'd better call Aunt Madge.*

The water boiled and I poured it into a teapot and got out the bowl that has several kinds of teabags. Ramona walked in as I put the bowl on the table with a mug.

"Oh, good. You feel like tea." She looked almost relieved.

"For you." I reached for the milkshake and she handed it to me. "This will help." I sat in one of the dinette chairs and she walked into the kitchen to bring back the teapot and a potholder to place it on. She poured a cup without saying anything as I sipped the wonderfully cold chocolate shake.

"This hits the spot." I smiled at her. "I'm tired of crying. Whatever's going to happen, I don't need a stuffed nose and headache."

She smiled, but looked somewhat uneasy. "I wonder if something has already happened."

"What do you mean?"

Ramona picked up the plastic bag that she'd brought in with the milkshake. She pulled out a small box and held it up. It said "Home Pregnancy Test."

I spit some milkshake on the table. "I don't *think* so!"

She spoke quietly. "Do you know? I mean, you can get pregnant right? And you aren't on the pill."

Sometimes people know a bit more about me than I might want. "I use a diaphragm. Same as you."

"Right. And they aren't perfect. Especially if you forget once."

I thought about that, and my face reddened as I remembered a weekend in mid-September. That was more than six weeks ago. *Whoa!* My confusion surely showed. "What made you think about this? Did Scoobie...?"

"God, no. You said your stomach had been upset. And you hardly every cry. And, um, your pants look a little tight."

"I have a good reason to be upset."

"You do. But what does it hurt to be sure?"

THIRTY MINUTES LATER, after a lot more crying and throwing up my milkshake, I sat calmly on the couch. *What will be will be.*

Ramona handed me a glass of ice water. "Congratulations."

I took it. "Not the way I planned it." *I might have to be a single mom.*

"No. But you remember the girl who had the lead in our senior class play?"

"Nope. I wasn't there for twelfth grade, remember?"

"Right. Well, she and her husband have been trying for four years. So, maybe you got…lucky."

I thought about that. "I like kids. I'd planned on being married when I got pregnant, not ditched by the man I love."

Ramona laughed. "He's been crazy about you since the first day he saw you."

I smiled. "You don't know that."

"It happens I do. Remember the day?"

"Yeah, he stopped me outside the principal's office..."

She was shaking her head. "No. He met you at First Prez the Sunday before that."

I sat up straighter. "That's right? How did you...?"

"I knew him better than you did back then. He kept asking me for tips to get to know you better."

I blanched. "No! How come I didn't...he was my best friend that year."

She nodded. "He was. And you needed a best friend more than a boyfriend in junior year. Remember how mad you were that your parents dumped you with your Aunt Madge for the school year?"

"Oh boy do I." I thought for a minute. "Best thing that ever happened to me."

"It'll all work out," she said, softly. "You guys'll figure it out."

I straightened my shoulders more. "Right. We will." I suddenly felt calmer. It was my job to figure this out. Mine and Scoobie's.

CHAPTER TWENTY-TWO

I HAD ALL DAY to do nothing but think. Except that I had a lot of appraisal work to do. I knew once I got busy my mind would stop the continual feedback loop of what-will-Scoobie-do, what-will-I-do?

I called Harry and Aunt Madge to apologize. Separately, they accepted my words with what I thought of as cool reserve. I hadn't called Mrs. Hardy yet. I dreaded it.

Going to the office would mean facing Harry's strong disapproval. I'd earned it. *Maybe I can beat him to the office.*

I was at Steele Appraisals by eight fifteen, which was very early for me. The house was quiet and cold. The thermostat said sixty-six, so I moved it to sixty-eight and appreciated the warmth that came with the whoosh from the vent.

A check of the fax showed one of Lester's more charming notes. "Harry, what planet are you from? Real estate prices are different here. Call me about the cottage on F Street."

I turned on the computer and was soon absorbed in giving the software instructions to draw a floor plan for the last house I'd visited, a small colonial.

The doorbell rang and I stretched and walked to the hallway. I parted the curtain on the door and was surprised to see Connie, the fairly new food pantry customer.

When she saw me she smiled broadly, held up a single pink carnation and spoke so I would hear her through the door. "I wanted to say thank you."

Connie had asked where I worked. I wasn't sure I liked the idea of someone I knew so little about appearing at the appraisal office, but it seemed really rude not to open the door.

As she walked in, I closed the door and said, "You really didn't have to thank me like this. I'm happy to be able to..." I stopped. Connie had turned to face me and was pointing a very small gun at me. *Is that real?*

Her smile was gone, replaced with something like a sneer. "Oh, I'm grateful. Grateful that you're going to take me to the rest of the money Joe owes me."

At my surely puzzled look, she added, "And it's Benji, not Connie."

"Oh, damn."

"Come on Jolie. I followed you to the hospital that day you visited Joe. He stayed at your aunt's place, and then I saw you talk to him, sitting really close at the table in his coffee place. You're real pals."

"You followed me to the hospital?"

"You drive like an old lady. Didn't get to the elevator in time. Couldn't find you in a room."

I remembered how miserable the weather was the second time I drove to Neptune. I had driven slowly, and a couple of cars stayed in my wake most of the way. I thought they were also cautious drivers in the rain.

Connie...Benji pointed the gun at me. "Come on. Where is it?"

"I didn't know anything about him having money until the day you took my niece. He denied having it many times."

"I believe you about as much as I believed him."

"You talked to Joe?"

She laughed, and it was a grating sound, with no mirth. "I don't like to show my face as much as dear Barry did. I also wear gloves when I'm hunting. Barry didn't, the fool."

I stared at her. All this time I'd thought Benji, whoever she was, sounded like the victim of a bullying boyfriend. "I can't show you a pile of money. How can I convince you of a negative?"

She didn't take her gaze off me, but I could tell she was thinking about what to do. She seemed to make a decision. "We're going back to Joe's apartment. It has to be..."

"No one will let us in there!"

"You have a key. I saw you use it last night." She gestured toward the door with her gun.

"If you were watching from somewhere last night, you might have noticed I was at the police station for almost two hours. They didn't exactly let me keep the key."

She regarded me with suspicion, and I added, "It wasn't mine. It belonged to the woman who owned the house, and she didn't know that I had it."

"So, get it again."

I gave her what I hoped was a withering look. "Oh, sure. She'll give me a key after I was with the guy who got shot on her steps."

Benji's face reddened. "Well think of something! There was at least another thirty thousand dollars. A few days ago I didn't have enough money for food. I want the rest of what Joe took."

"Thirty thousand!" I had never known how much was taken. It was likely in some newspaper article in Kansas, but I'd never seen it.

"That's my money." She almost snarled. "I planned that robbery. Joe didn't have a record, so we hid the money at his place. Cops would never have found it there. But Joe was a pansy. When Barry got arrested, Joe freaked. I never pegged him for a thief or I would've hid it better." Her face was now so red it looked about to explode.

Benji's face explosion would have been okay with me, but it wasn't likely. "I'm thinking. What if..." I didn't really have a what if to offer, but gave it a stab. "Maybe he had a safe deposit box."

"Like I could get in there. Where'd he stash the money in the store?"

"It was a perfect spot. He put in a fake thermostat when he remodeled, after the hurricane. It was hollow behind the thermostat face."

"Then there's another fake place."

I tried to calm myself. "If there is, the only way we'll find it is to go to Java Jolt."

Benji raised her wrist and glanced at a watch. "Too busy in there now. I walked by there a lot. Wanted to get Joe alone, but that old lady dropped him off and a couple of you were always with him when he left."

She's talking about Aunt Madge! I can't let her hurt Aunt Madge.

"We'll go at nine-thirty. That George guy will probably be the only one there. If you two behave I won't hurt you. Or those cute little girls." She gestured toward the living room couch. "Sit."

I didn't ask her if I should bark. Instead, I sat and brooded while Benji paced from the living room across the entry foyer, into the office, and back to the living room. I wasn't about to try something stupid like tackling her. I realized that since Benji had arrived I hadn't thought about being pregnant. *Another reason not to do anything rash.*

My mobile phone was with the police. If I could get to the house phone to call 9-1-1, the police would know the address, even if I didn't have time to say a word. But would a successful call enrage Benji so much that she would use that gun? I figured even a small gun made a big hole.

A car door slammed. My glance toward the window led Benji to look out.

"Damn it to hell!" She gesture with her gun. "Get up. We go out the back fast and I won't have to hurt your boss."

I stood and moved quickly toward the back door, Benji just behind me. I didn't hear the front door open, but thought I heard Harry call my name as Benji and I moved onto the porch.

She poked me in the back. "Move it. Your car."

I walked, but said, "My keys are in my purse, in the house."

Benji let loose a long string of expletives, followed by, "Walk toward the beach."

I complied, longing to glance over my shoulder to see Harry peering out the back door.

"Faster," she hissed. "Turn on Ferry, toward the ocean."

I did as she said, realizing that it would only take about five minutes to get to the boardwalk, a couple more to get to

Java Jolt. If only I could call attention to myself. Maybe trip on the curb...

"You're slowing down, Jolie."

"Sorry." *I can't believe I apologized to her.*

The four blocks from Ferry to the boardwalk were residential except for a sub shop on the corner of Ferry and C Streets. No one I knew would pass by in a car. However, when we got to the boardwalk, we'd have to walk along it, or else walk parallel to it on B Street. A lot of cars would go by us. Benji and I were walking close enough to each other that we were obviously together, but one behind the other. Maybe someone would think that peculiar and take a closer look.

As we got to C Street, Benji said, "Walk left. We're going to your food place."

"Why?" *Is it a quiet place to kill me?*

"Since you ask nice, because that coffee place will still have too many people in it, so we need a place to wait. People expect to see you at the food pantry. And you better have that key."

"Okay." I pictured Harvest for All in my head. I knew the layout well and Benji didn't. How could I use that to advantage? There were a sharp pair of metal scissors and a couple small knives under the counter. I often used them to open boxes, but I didn't think I could force myself to stab anyone with them.

A rest room was just outside the pantry, in the hall by the First Prez community room. No window, but I thought the door had a lock. If I could get in there ahead of Benji...

A car horn blasted about twenty feet from us, and Aunt Madge put down her car window. "I thought you were going to take it easy today."

"I am. Just taking a walk." I took in her orange hair, now minus its black streak, and the bright yellow scarf at her neck. I hoped orange wasn't the last hair color I would see her in.

Another car beeped behind Aunt Madge, and she pulled back into traffic.

I had wanted to tell her to get the police, but no way would I put her in danger. With a sinking feeling I realized that Harry had not spotted anything amiss at the appraisal office. If he had, he would have called Aunt Madge and she'd have jumped out of the car to ask me why I left Harry's back door open.

We were almost at the church when a police cruiser came toward us. The driver took one hand off the steering wheel for a moment and gave a short wave, palm facing me in the sort of greeting Native Americans make and say "how." In the movies anyway.

"Don't you do anything," Benji said.

As the car drew even with us I recognized Dana and waved back. I wondered if she could tell my hand was shaking. She passed us.

We were almost to the food pantry door when I realized I didn't have the key. It was on the same ring as my car keys. My response to Benji had been automatic. *She isn't going to like this.*

We reached the Harvest for All door. I half turned to tell her I didn't have the key, when a man's voice yelled, "It's open." It sounded like Reverend Jamison.

"Get rid of the priest," Benji said, barely louder than a whisper.

"He's a reverend."

"I don't care if he's the president, make him leave."

I pushed open the door, but before I could say hello, Reverend Jamison looked up and smiled as he spoke. "Father Teehan wanted to see the volunteer list. I told him he could as long as he...oh, hello." He nodded to Benji. "I didn't realize Jolie had anyone with her."

Benji morphed into Connie, complete with wide smile. "Jolie's going to tell me more about what you do here."

"Never a dull moment," he said, and patted the pocket of his slacks, pulled out his phone, and glanced at it. "I've got to take this. Back in a moment." He walked out the pantry door that went to the church rather than the street.

The door had barely pulled shut behind him when Sergeant Morehouse and Officer Curly Hair stood from behind the counter, pointing guns at Benji. I had the good sense to squat.

"Keep your hands at your sides or I'll shoot," Morehouse said. When she didn't move, he jerked his head toward his companion. "Corporal."

Benji swore, but she stayed put.

Officer Curly Hair put his gun back in its holster and removed a pair of handcuffs from his belt.

I crawled a few feet closer to the counter and looked up. Benji's expression was one of utter fury, but she kept her hands at her sides until the corporal took first the right one and put it in a handcuff, then the left.

As he began to frisk her, Benji glared down at me. "What did you do, you bitch?"

Morehouse holstered his gun, walked quickly around the counter, and extended a hand to help me up. "You'll want to send Harry a thank-you note."

CHAPTER TWENTY-THREE

I WOULDN'T LET Sergeant Morehouse call Scoobie, but Aunt Madge didn't ask, she just did it.

"He says one of the other radiology techs is sick, and he needs to stay at the hospital, unless you really, really need him." She was sitting next to me in the police department's small conference room. For the moment we were alone.

"Did you tell him it wasn't my fault?"

"Lieutenant Tortino had already called him to say you were all right, in case Scoobie heard about it from someone else. I doubt the lieutenant said you went looking for the woman."

"So, when Harry realized something was wrong, he called you?"

"Police first, I think. I was driving to the appraisal office when I saw you. Harry saw that woman's back as you were leaving the house. I guess her fingerprints had already turned up somewhere, so the police figured who it was and fanned out to look for you. It was incredibly fortunate that the sergeant had just gone to First Prez to see if you were in the food pantry."

I was about to ask her if Reverend Jamison was part of a quick plan to get me into Harvest for All, but footsteps in the hall said we were getting company again.

Morehouse walked back into the room and stared at me for a second. "You sure know how to pick 'em." He sat across from me.

I did my best to glare, but it's not easy when you're trying to keep your lips sort of pursed so you don't cry. "Not funny."

He ignored my rebuke. "She mighta been in town as long as Belken was. She's not talking."

I remembered what Dana had told me. "Maybe Benji was driving the car. The one that crashed outside Markle's store."

Morehouse's tone was sharp. "Why would you think that?"

Nuts. I can't blame Aunt Madge's network. "I thought I heard that Belken's prints were in the car, but not on the steering wheel."

Morehouse rubbed his face for a moment and then picked up his pen from the table. "If I find out who told you that she's in trouble."

"Mostly men work here."

He snorted. "What else can you tell me?"

It was almost an hour before I could leave, and all I wanted was a nap.

Aunt Madge started her car as I shut the passenger door. She turned toward me and I met her gaze. "If you hadn't left your purse and car at the appraisal office, Harry wouldn't have known you were in any trouble."

I nodded. "And I am in trouble."

Ground to a Halt

SCOOBIE'S CAR PULLED into the drive at three forty-five. I had placed a banana and bowl on the kitchen counter and paced the living room at least fifteen times in the past twenty minutes.

The key turned in the front door. *Why didn't I open it? He'll think I don't want to see him! Stop over-thinking everything.*

The door opened and our eyes met. "Hey," I said.

"Hey yourself." His tone was reserved, but not angry.

That's a good sign.

His expression relaxed. "Morehouse called me about half an hour ago. He seemed to think you wanted me to know you didn't go looking for that woman." He took his backpack off his shoulder and walked up and gave me the barest of pecks on the cheek. "I'm glad you're safe, but we still have last night to deal with."

I walked into the kitchen and picked up the banana and bowl to show him.

He looked amused. "Man, you really are trying to get on my good side."

"Yep. You want me to warm this up while you change?"

"Sure."

I mashed the banana and put it in the microwave for the required twenty seconds. The peanut butter I would leave to him.

Pebbles followed Scoobie into the kitchen and Jazz stood at the edge of the room. She had never seen me so upset, not even when I left my gambling husband and fled to Ocean Alley. It seemed to make her nervous.

I fed Pebbles while Scoobie finished making his concoction and we walked to the living room together. He sat on the couch, and I sat across from him. It sort of felt as if sitting next to him would be presumptuous.

After he'd taken a couple of bites, I said, "I'm not sure where to start."

"It's not going to be easy. We've been over some of...this before," Scoobie said.

I nodded. "You've asked me to mind my own business a lot of times."

He shook his head slightly. "It's not so much that."

"It's that I lied," I said, softly.

"It is." He looked around the living room. "Where's that list you dropped on the floor this morning?"

"Oh. You saw it." I stood and reached under a couch cushion, pulled it out, and handed it to him.

"Hiding it?"

I sat back down. "Not really. I keep remembering more to add, so I'm keeping it close."

He kind of grunted a laugh as he read, then looked at me. "Pretty comprehensive list."

I frowned. "I'm sure I'll think of more."

He patted the couch cushion next to him and I moved to sit there. We leaned back, shoulders touching.

"The thing is," Scoobie said, "I don't want you to think you have to kiss my ass for a week. It's just I really can't...go through something like this again."

I nodded. "On top of the deception I could have been killed."

"Yeah. Am I on your life insurance yet?"

I nudged him in the elbow. "Jazz gets it all."

"None for Pebbles?"

"She makes too big a mess in her litter box."

"Good a criterion as any, I guess." He reached his arm around my shoulder and pulled me closer. I put my head on his shoulder and curled my legs under me.

"So," I asked. "Are we okay?"

"I think so. As long as we're always honest with each other. I can't really afford to date anyone else until I pay off my student loans."

I let out a breath and pulled a little away from him, so I could look him in the eyes. "There's an especially good reason for us to be glad about that."

"The not dating part?" His grin was catching, and I smiled.

"Ramona brought me a milkshake this morning."

He rolled his eyes. "George said he was going to call her. I told him to mind his own beeswax."

"He's not very good at that."

Scoobie leaned his head back and laughed for several seconds, and then wiped his eyes. "Do you realize how wrong it is that you think that?"

I grinned. "It's part of my learning experience." I grew more serious. "It was good to see her. She, uh, brought me something else?"

"From her trip, you mean?"

"Uh, no. She was sort of concerned that my stomach was upset."

"Are you sick?" Scoobie asked.

"Oh, no." I looked at him. "I guess because she'd been away...when I said coffee had been bothering me..."

Scoobie looked bemused, then he sat up straighter. "What did she bring you?"

I swallowed. "A pregnancy test."

Color drained from his face. I felt bile rise in my throat. "We're going to be parents."

"Oh, wow." He stared at me, and then stood. "I need to go outside for a minute." He walked out.

"Oh, no." I wasn't sure whether I'd said it out loud. I stood, too, and walked to the kitchen and back, then around the living room.

The front door opened and Scoobie came in and closed it. Our eyes met, and he gestured to the couch. "Have a seat."

He has some color back, that's a good thing.

He sat next to me and took my hand. "The thing is, I thought this would be really different."

"Me, too," I whispered.

He opened his other hand, which held some grass. Then he dropped to one knee. "Jolie Gentil, will you marry me?"

My eyes flooded. I couldn't help it. "But, were we, we really, do you feel...?" I couldn't make myself say *trapped*.

"Come on, Jolie. We were always going to spend our lives together. I just knew it before you did."

I wiped my eyes. "Ramona told me you asked for tips when you met me."

"Ah yes, Ramona and her mouth."

I smiled at him. "Yes. Yes I will marry you."

He got up and sat next to me. "You could have said it faster. My knee hurts." He took my hand, and slipped the hastily woven grass ring on my finger.

"Oh." I studied it and then looked at him, grinning. "How can I preserve it?"

"I've been saving for another kind of ring since I got my job."

"I don't need another kind of ring."

"I know."

He pulled me toward him and we kissed for a long time.

We opened our eyes and I started to giggle.

"Ramona knew before either of us," I said.

"So, is she godmother?" he teased.

I shook my head. "Renée. Do we need George for godfather?"

"That would only encourage your snooping. You know what we do need?"

I shook my head.

"A bigger house."

I'm all for that.

CAST OF CHARACTERS

Alicia Ortiz – local high school student, daughter of Megan

Andrew - married to Jolie's sister, Renée

Aretha Brown – not the least bit shy Harvest for All committee member

Aunt Madge – best aunt ever, sister to Jolie's late grandmother

Connie -- Harvest for All customer

Daphne – librarian and high school classmate of Jolie and Scoobie

Dr. Welby – retired doctor and member, Harvest for All Committee

Father Teehan – pastor of St. Anthony's

George Winters – former reporter at *Ocean Alley Press*, now an insurance investigator

Harry Steele – owner of Steele Appraisals, and Aunt Madge's husband

Jennifer Stenner – owns the other appraisal firm, mentioned only once in this book

Joe Regan – owner of Java Jolt, local coffee house

Jolie Gentil – Ocean Alley real estate appraiser with a nose for trouble

Harvest for All – food pantry for which Jolie chairs the governing committee

Julia - Renée and Andrew's daughter, Jolie's niece

Lance Wilson – Jolie's favorite member of the Harvest for All Committee

Lester Argrow – annoying local real estate agent, and Ramona's uncle

Lieutenant Tortino – member of the Ocean Alley Police Department

Max – friendly but brain-damaged Iraq War veteran who likes Jolie and Scoobie
Megan Ortiz – regular volunteer at Harvest for All food pantry
Michele - Renée and Andrew's daughter, Jolie's niece
Mr. Markle – owner of In-Town Grocery who is good to the food pantry
Monica Martin – very shy Harvest for All committee member
Sergeant Morehouse – member of the Ocean Alley Police Department
Ramona Argrow – clerk at the Purple Cow office supply store, and Jolie's friend
Renée -- Jolie's sister
Reverend Douglas Jamison – clergyman for First Presbyterian
Ronald - nurse at a local hospital
Scoobie – Jolie's best bud, just finished school to become a radiology tech
Sylvia Parrett – Harvest for All committee member, who can be a tad grouchy
Talbot Peters - helps at Java Jolt for a time
Tiffany –reporter at the *Ocean Alley Press*

ABOUT THE AUTHOR

Elaine L. Orr is the Amazon bestselling author of *Trouble on the Doorstep* and other books in the Jolie Gentil cozy mystery series, which now has eight books and a prequel. She wrote plays and novellas for years and graduated to longer fiction. *Biding Time*, was one of five finalists in the National Press Club's first fiction contest, in 1993. She is a regular attendee at conferences such as Muncie's Midwest Writers Workshop and Magna Cum Murder, and conducts presentations on electronic publishing and other writing-related topics. Her nonfiction includes carefully researched local and family history books. Elaine grew up in Maryland and moved to the Midwest in 1994.

* * * * *

The eight books and prequel to the Jolie Gentil Cozy Mystery Series are:

Appraisal for Murder
Rekindling Motives
When the Carny Comes to Town
Any Port in a Storm
Trouble on the Doorstep
Behind the Walls
Vague Images
Ground to a Halt
And the prequel:
Jolie and Scoobie High School Misadventures

Scoobie's poetry is that of real-life poet, James W. Larkin.
www.elaineorr.com
www.elaineorr.blogspot.com